CRUSOES
OF THE PRAIRIE

Written and Illustrated by
DON HILLSON

(Author of "THE FORT IN THE FOREST,"
"THE RANCH ON THE PLAIN")

SCHOFIELD & SIMS LTD.
HUDDERSFIELD

Made and Printed in Great Britain

CONTENTS

CHAPTER I

MOUSIE

"It was *not* my fault!" said Dick Warner sullenly, still heated with his battle. "All I did was to tell Redfeather to stop ill-treating that grey colt."

"But, Dick! Redfeather—the Chief's son!" His sister May, aged twelve, was too sun-tanned to turn pale, but her eyes expressed her alarm. As for Tony, their small brother, his eyelashes glistened with moisture. Not five minutes ago he had cheered when the young Redskin had gone head over heels into the dust, reeling from a straight left from Dick, but now, having had time to think, all three were alarmed.

The old squaw, with whom they lived, had made matters worse by shrieking angrily, "You'll all be burnt at the stake! Had you no more sense, Deek, than to strike Arrowhead's son?"

"You are only trying to scare us," said Dick, touching his cut lip. "I tell you he struck first! Sprang on me like a catamount—isn't a fellow allowed to defend himself?"

"You'll lose your scalps for this," gritted out the squaw, leaning forward to where the three sat huddled together on a pile of skins at the rear of the wigwam, and, seizing Tony's curls, made a horrible motion of scalping him and waving imaginary hair.

5

"For shame, Granny," said May, cuddling Tony to her bosom. "It serves Redfeather jolly well right. He's a cruel, sly, boastful——"

"What did he do?" broke in the squaw, kneeling again to her rug making.

"Tried to ride that unbroken colt," answered fourteen-year-old Dick. "Half strangled him with a rope round his neck and then stabbed him with a spear because he pranced about. He'll spoil Mousie —that's the name I've given the colt because of his colour, although he's wild as a lynx—but not with me—why?—because I was brought up among horses and understand them."

The three captives had been adopted by the squaw when her own two sons had died, and she liked them and did not want them to get into trouble. Dick, May and Tony, for their part, had now become resigned to their fate. The four seasons had passed since they had been surprised when picnicking among the foothills near their ranch, and carried off by a Pawnee war party, and they had wandered with Arrowhead's tribe so far afield that all sense of direction had been lost. Now, except for their fair hair and blue eyes, they would have passed for Indian children: dress, speech, habits and as copper-skinned as the natives. Dick and Tony wore loin cloths, but May had woven a dress with the help of the old squaw they called Gran. After the shock of capture had passed away, they had been fairly happy, except when in dreams they lived again in Riverside

Ranch, and on awakening, the torment in their eyes betrayed their thoughts, but neither Dick nor May ever spoke to Tony of their dreams.

Now there was trouble because of Mousie. As Dick sat sewing beads to the seam of his leather riding trousers he recalled how he had ridden with the Braves to round up the drove of wild horses. What a ten mile kicking scrimmage it had been, how enjoyable, and how cunningly the Redskins had corralled them. Dick had noticed Mousie the colt, and taken a fancy to him, and while his jet-black mother had been broken in by a warrior, Dick had partly gentled the son, patiently winning the colt's trust by kindness. Very few of the Indian boys dare approach Mousie, and Redfeather, the Chief's son, had become jealous.

Then, that same morning when Redfeather had attempted to straddle Mousie and been thrown, he had attacked him with a spear and twisted his rawhide lasso until the colt squealed for breath.

Hearing the hubbub, Dick had rushed to the corral and told Redfeather to let Mousie go. Redfeather, hot with rage, had struck Dick who had retaliated by knocking the Chief's son head over heels.

A shadow darkened the wigwam opening and a young Brave looked in and crooked a finger to Dick. Tony clung to his brother's arm and May looked scared, but Dick Warner faced punishment with calm courage.

"Oh! Don't you worry, sister. Arrowhead growls a lot but won't bite. I'll soon be back."

Arrowhead, the Head Chief, was sitting cross-legged in his large teepee, smoking through the handle of his tomahawk. When he acted as Judge for the tribe he wore his magnificent war-bonnet of eagle feathers. His face was stern set and expressionless. Standing beside him was Redfeather, a sneer on his lips, a look which said plainer than words, "My Dad's a Chief—now you're for it."

Arrowhead called out a gruff order and a dozen blooded warriors filed into the wigwam and stood respectfully at attention; all wore head-dresses feathered according to the number of brave deeds they had done.

"White Boy," said Arrowhead, fixing his black

piercing eyes on Dick, "prepare to die. To-day you have struck the son of your Chief. Is that true?"

"It is, Great Chief," Dick answered calmly although, truth to tell, his bare knees felt wobbly and his pulses throbbed with real alarm. He knew Arrowhead's heart was flint hard and his nature savage as a wolf. During Dick's year of captivity he had heard captives shrieking at the stake as the fire consumed their limbs; remembered other horrible nights when painted warriors, worked up to a frenzy, danced the war dance. At such times he, May and Tony had sat shivering in their teepee, for when lusting for battle, Braves sometimes wreaked their vengeance on white captives.

"Is it true that you struck my son first?" asked the Chief, fixing Dick with a snakish eye.

"No, O' Chief," he replied. "Redfeather struck——"

"I didn't!" burst out the Indian lad, his eyes flashing as he sprang truculently in front of Dick, but at a sign from Arrowhead, a Brave pulled Redfeather back.

"Stand behind me, son!" barked the Chief, and like a dog coming to heel the youth obeyed the order. Arrowhead had already received a full account from witnesses of what had happened.

"Then prepare to receive Big Owl's knife," announced Arrowhead, and immediately a tall Brave stepped forward, and slipping a keen-edged knife from his belt, began to sharpen the edge on his buckskin trousers. *Wheet, wheet*! scraped the blade—a terrifying sound.

Arrowhead drew at his pipe. "Stand behind the White Boy, Chief Big Owl," he ordered, "and at my third puff—*strike*! and let one blow be enough."

The ring of warriors looked calmly on, not a change of expression on the dozen faces, except that of Redfeather who, behind his father's back, still gloated.

This was the first time Dick had been brought before Arrowhead and he almost gave himself up for lost, but pride of race steeled his heart. He would die like a Paleface. A vision of his mother, of Rancher Warner, the cowboys, his pets, May and little Tony waiting for his return—a succession of pictures flashed into his mind. . . .

"One," said Arrowhead with a puff of smoke.

"Two," another puff.

"*Three*!"

Dick closed his eyes; and then, finding himself still alive, opened them again. Nothing had altered.

"Wah!" said Arrowhead. "The White Boy has courage . . . it is good . . . but why did he steal my son's colt?"

"I have not stolen Mousie—I mean the colt," Dick replied. "It belongs to no one."

"It is mine!" called out Redfeather. "Did I not ride him this morning?"

"You rode him swift as arrow from bow," said Dick, speaking in the Indian way. "One minute on —the next flying like a—um!—red feather blown by the wind."

Warriors seldom show their feelings, but at that moment several mouths twitched and even Arrowhead's eyes twinkled. He rubbed an eyeball, pretending smoke had filtered there. "Can you ride—er— what does the White Boy call the colt?"

"Mousie."

"Wah! Mousie, because it is timid. Can you ride a timid mouse?"

"I have tried," Dick admitted.

"And can you, son Redfeather?"

"Yes, easily."

"Then we will have a test before the assembled tribe," Arrowhead went on. "The Mouse shall be brought out at sundown and whoever rides him longest shall win one honour feather and keep the colt. Big Owl—at sunset these boys shall draw the pebble for first attempt. I have spoken. You can go, White Boy."

CHAPTER II

THE PRIZE

WITH a weight lifted from his heart, Dick returned to his own wigwam. May and Tony were quite cheerful, having been told by the squaw that Arrowhead would only try to scare the White Boy. Dick danced a jig until, catching a toe in Gran's rug frame, he overbalanced and fell sprawling. He rose, sobered by his fall.

"I'll show him!" he cried joyfully, rubbing his hard arm muscles. "I'll show that crafty Redfeather who owns Mousie. I've already ridden him three times whereas he won't let Redfeather come near him. Hi-O! I'll win honour. I'll wear a head-ring and a feather in my cap, and not a red feather," he added in an undertone. "May I borrow your black dye, Gran, please?"

He slipped an arm round her gaudy shawl, and although looking pleased, she wriggled free, because to show affection was frowned on in the Pawnee camp.

"Don't count your 'possums before they're caught," answered Gran. "Fetch a gourd of water while Blossom lights a fire, and you, Ton-ie, off you go for sticks, and don't bring any elm or chestnut to set the teepee alight; bring beech or ash, they never spark; and take your pup for a run."

Dick Warner was in jolly mood, confident of success; for the riding contest he had put on his leather trousers in place of his shabby loin-cloth. Around him surged the whole Pawnee tribe: chattering squaws, calm faced warriors, children jigging and laughing with expectation. In the open space before Arrowhead's teepee sat a ring of under-chiefs, no one near them except the two competitors, seemingly friendly; yet fear and hatred lurked in the Indian lad's heart: he knew the mouse-grey colt and was trembling inwardly.

At sunset Arrowhead stalked out of his teepee and a hush fell over the assembled tribe. Behind him came his squaw and her three boys all older than Redfeather. One of them carried an embroidered head-ring with a solitary feather attached—the first step to warrior rank.

At a shout from Big Owl, second in command, Dick and Redfeather came running up. Arrowhead held out his closed fists in one of which was a pebble. "Choose!" he ordered gruffly. Dick let Redfeather have the first choice and then touched Arrowhead's other hand. "Wah!" grunted the Chief, opening them. "My son wins."

All eyes now turned to the rodeo ground and through a gap in the crowd came the prancing colt, blindfolded with a blanket, yet lively enough to give the Brave leading him plenty of trouble.

Mousie was a lovely animal, still leggy but well shaped; already his mouse colour was streaked with

black hairs foretelling his proper colour—black—
like his mother; half wild, he knew nothing of bridles
or bits to rasp the tongue; instead he wore a horse-
hair head-rope with a loop of rawhide around his
nose; on his back was a folded blanket with a leather
bag stuffed with hay, strapped securely to serve as a
saddle.

Arrowhead made a sign and the competitors stepped
into the ring to show themselves. Walking one on
either side of Mousie they made a circuit of the
crowd; then at a motion of Arrowhead's hand, Dick
ran back to May and Tony leaving Mousie alone in
the open space, pawing, snorting, nervous but, being
blindfolded, almost afraid to move.

The crowd was now agog with excitement, as
Redfeather, looking jauntier than he felt, ran lightly
up to Mousie, and seizing the head-rope, vaulted
into the saddle.

Mousie immediately reared on hind legs, working
his fore legs like a boxer, but being still blindfolded,
dare not run. There was no merit in such riding and
the crowd roared its displeasure. Squaws shook their
fists and screamed; children cat-called; Braves nodded
disgustedly one to another. Although frightened,
Redfeather took the hint and whisked the blanket
from Mousie's eyes.

For one instant the colt looked surprised, then,
startled by the roar of the crowd and angry at the
weight across his shoulders and the unaccustomed
rope round his tender nose, he began his tricks.

Up into the air he shot like a bouncing ball, fore legs pawing, dancing on his hind ones, then down to the turf with a thud of hoofs and a jar enough to break the rider's spine. Clutching head-rope and mane Redfeather hung on, marvelling at being able to stick there even for so short a time. Round the ring they went, Mousie seeming to have a score of legs; then with a sudden twist of his lithe body head to tail, he sent Redfeather sailing up towards the crimson sky.

Landing on hands and knees easily as a cat, the Chief's son rose and ran to his father expecting praise and eyeing the one-feather war-bonnet, but with a grunt Arrowhead waved him to one side. Secretly he had hoped to see his son 'taken down'; of late he had been a little above himself, conceited, boastful,

15

disobedient to his mother. Arrowhead was a hard father and entirely just, in no way favouring his own sons.

Although surprised at Redfeather's success, Dick knew he could do better. Mousie knew him and when in quiet mood had allowed him to mount and ride. Here was his chance, actually to *own* Mousie. All he had to do was to stick on longer than Redfeather; three minutes would win easily. With May and Tony by his side he awaited a sign from Arrowhead, but Indians are in no hurry. Redfeather had returned into the ring and was showing off, cartwheeling across in front of the colt and pretending to mount again, but being careful to keep away from his hoofs.

Suddenly the youth tightened the strap holding the blanket to Mousie's back. "That's kind of him," frowned Dick, "but he could have left it to me. Showing off—that's what he's doing because he kept on for two minutes."

Again the crowd quietened down as Arrowhead motioned to Dick to do his turn.

"Mousie," whispered Dick, as the ring of onlookers pressed back to give plenty of room, "as you love me and I love you, be as quiet as your name . . . then you'll be mine. I'll be your master and a kinder one you'll never want. We'll roam the prairie. . . . My! what fun we'll have," all the time rubbing his hands over Mousie's nose, letting him smell the familiar odour, and Mousie was delighted, whinnying with pleasure. His master was here—the good master who stroked and gentled him, rubbed him down and gave him chunks of maple sugar.

The eyes of the crowd were on the Young Paleface. Most of them wished he would win because Redfeather was not well liked, whereas the White Papooses were always ready to fetch or carry for the infirm squaws.

To show his mastery over the colt, Dick did not blindfold him; instead, taking a grip of the flowing mane, he vaulted on to his back.

Instantly he went sailing skyward as Mousie gave a wild shriek and sprang yards into the air: a cruel spur, a spear point could not have made him jump quicker. Dick was ready for a spring, but not for such a wild leap; no time to get a grip with strong knees. With a mighty wrench he saved himself from being unhorsed, but as he straddled the saddle again, once more Mousie leaped and roared with pain. . . .

Dick Warner picked himself up from the brown turf, knowing he was beaten. The crowd stood looking stolidly on, as surprised as the Paleface Boy. Many knew he could manage Mousie; had seen him riding along the forest glades, and now at the test he had been thrown off in half Redfeather's time.

That youth looked pleased as he ran up to his father.

Arrowhead rose from his log and the crowd grew silent. There was no doubt who had won the contest, and yet . . . many were puzzled. As though sorry at his behaviour the colt pranced round to Dick and thrust his muzzle into the boy's hands. Dick stroked the velvet nose and whispered, "Mousie, O Mousie, why *did* you do it? You are lost to me now. Goodbye, my pal. . . ."

The Chief was speaking: "I award the honour feather to my son Redfeather, and also the ownership of the grey colt. Let the tribe make note of it. Down on one knee, son, while I fit your head-ring. As for the Paleface Boy, he did his best and as reward shall keep the blanket and saddle."

Dick accepted the prizes with a bow, and turning sadly away, pushed through the crowd to where May and Tony were waiting.

CHAPTER III

REDFEATHER'S TRICKERY

"WHAT a pity!" said the sister, as they walked back to their wigwam. "And how queerly Mousie behaved."

"Anyway," said Dick, "I was beaten so I'll make no excuses. Here's a fine present for you, Gran," placing the folded blanket into her hands.

The old squaw was sorry Dick had lost the contest, but smiled as she accepted the gift. It would save her hours of labour, and she was stroking the folds with obvious delight when of a sudden she gave a little cry and eyed her palm now red with blood.

Instantly she turned with a cry of rage and shook her fist at the children. "You worthless set of Palefaces," she gritted out, "to trick an old woman so—for shame!" She aimed a flat-handed blow at Dick who avoided it with ease.

"Heh! Wait a moment, Gran," he cried. "What's the matter?"

"You've stuck a needle through the folds—you bad boy."

"I'm sure I didn't."

"Then it was Blossom."

"I wouldn't do such a foolish trick," May denied swiftly.

"Then it must be my little Ton-ie. Was it you?" She shook a finger at the wide-eyed child.

"No, Gran."

Suddenly Dick sprang forward, his eyes alight as he placed a hand carefully on the blanket and pressed downwards, and the group gave a little cry as several long thorns, strong and sharp as needles came through the black stripe and disappeared when Dick took away the pressure.

For several seconds all were too amazed and disgusted to speak; then Dick ejaculated, "Well! Of all the deceitful, crafty fellows——"

"No wonder Mousie jumped," said May.

"He'll suffer for this," said Dick grimly, watching Gran carefully lift fold after fold until, above the bottom layer, there appeared a twig of thorn with wicked-looking prongs. May was about to remove it when the squaw stopped her.

"Leave it," she warned, covering it with a fold of blanket. "Arrowhead shall know about this."

"Who do you think did it?" asked May.

Gran placed a finger alongside her nose and looked sly. "The one who profits by it, of course."

"Redfeather?" queried May disgustedly.

"No one else touched Mousie, after the Brave led him into the ring," said Dick, "but it would be difficult to prove Redfeather put the thorns there."

"But aren't you going to tell Arrowhead?" asked May.

"Now really, sister, how could I? It would be too

much like making an excuse. I should appear a bad loser."

"Then I'll go and tell him," said May with spirit. "We are not going to allow you to be cheated. . . . Ah! Where's Gran going?"

"I go to Big Owl's teepee," she replied. "He will tell Arrowhead. Don't touch that blanket."

Big Owl's beady eyes shone with understanding as he realised the trick. He had returned with Gran whom he liked, and the squaw had invited him to sit down and smoke a pipe. Big Owl had soon sprung up again. "He has the cunning of a wolverine," he remarked, "and had not his father given the blanket to Deek, no one would have known. I will take the blanket at once to Arrowhead."

The short twilight had settled over the encampment. The forest edge showed grape-purple against the daffodil sky. Teepees formed dark triangles, with some of their openings showing a dull flickering orange from the fires within.

The Warner children and the squaw sat by their teepee opening looking along the double line of wigwams, all decorated with pictures—a deer, a bison, a racoon, or other distinguishing mark.

At the sound of voices they looked in the opposite direction and saw Mousie being led in by Redfeather from the horse lines. Half a dozen youths followed.

Redfeather halted at sight of the group in the wigwam opening and, standing erect, touched his headdress proudly and meaningly. None of them took any notice of him, staring past the youths towards the distant forest. The sight of Mousie decorated with a necklace of red feathers gave Dick a stab at the heart; but for May's restraining hand he would have risen and smote the conceited Redfeather to the earth. Perhaps the Chief's son guessed as much, for with a sneer and a low remark heard only by his mates but which made them guffaw, he walked on again.

"The air seems sweeter," sniffed Gran, loud enough for all to hear, "now the skunk has passed," and Redfeather knew what she meant.

For a time they sat in the cool darkness watching a strange scene take place in front of the Chief's teepee. They saw Redfeather hand Mousie's rope to a youth to hold while he went inside. Then the scene changed as torches were lighted and two Braves came out and stood beside the colt. He shied at the light and had to be blindfolded. Arrowhead appeared and stood, arms folded, watching while a Brave held a torch close to Mousie's back looking carefully as though searching. When he touched certain spots on the animal's hide Mousie shuddered as though with pain.

"He's looking for thorn points," said Dick. "I guess some broke off and if not taken out poor Mousie will have a sore back. Anyway, it will prove—— Hullo! Here comes Eagle Eye."

A youth came running up and said the Chief wanted to speak to the Paleface Boy.

Once more Dick stood before Arrowhead. In the

orange flare of the torches, the place looked weird; Braves stood looking on, among them Big Owl who stared so long at Dick without speaking that he grew nervous. To strike Redfeather as he had done that morning was a small offence, but to accuse him of cheating, of being 'snake tongued' was serious. Amongst themselves Redskins take pride in being strictly honest.

Dick was worried, knowing what was coming. Arrowhead was giving him time to think. The Chief knew his son was conceited and none too brave, but never imagined he would stoop to rascality—to be a cheat.

"Come nearer," said Arrowhead, crooking a finger. Dick stepped forward until the smoke from the tomahawk rose almost directly under his nose. This was no joking matter he knew. Arrowhead's eyes glittered in the light from the flickering torches, making his high cheek bones glisten, his long curved nose look sharp-edged; the feathers on his war-bonnet gleamed golden with blood-red tips; other Chiefs wore tall war-bonnets; behind stood the three sons, but the squaw was not there. A little apart was Redfeather and his supporters, there for a purpose Dick could guess.

Now indeed he faced death in some horrible form, but a sense of injustice rankling in his heart gave him courage and a calm dignified bearing. He *had* been cheated and would not back out. He would answer truthfully and face punishment like a Paleface.

"The White Boy lost the contest," said Arrowhead. "Isn't that so?"

"It is, Great Chief."

"Is he satisfied with my verdict?"

Dick hesitated. Life was good; he had been fairly content as a captive and there was always the chance of escape—some day. If he died, May and Tony would be alone. He thought of them—waiting—of his parents—the Ranch. Was ever a boy in such a desperate fix? If he said, "Yes, O' Chief, I am satisfied," all would be well. But to say, "No. . . ."

Dare he?

The Warners were a God-fearing family, and although outwardly the three captives had to listen to the Medicine Man's nonsense, in secret they still whispered, "Our Father . . ." at dead of night when the old squaw slept. "And deliver us from evil, for Thine is the kingdom, the Power . . ." As Dick stood wavering, the words were ringing through his brain. "The Power . . ." Had God the Power to save him? Inside the teepee there was silence, but from the forest came the cry of a night bird. It reminded Dick of St. Peter when at night he denied his Lord to the Roman soldiers. Squaring his shoulders he looked Arrowhead straight in the eyes and said, "I am *not* satisfied, Great Chief. Someone placed sharp thorns in the blanket."

"Who?" barked Arrowhead.

"I . . . don't know, but whoever it was . . . was told to do so by *him*." He pointed an accusing finger at Redfeather.

The Chief's son looked amazed and the Braves murmured angrily.

"Have you anything more to say?" asked Arrowhead.

"No, Chief."

"Then listen, White Boy," Arrowhead pointed his pipe stem and then began puffing again. "You have made a serious accusation. Only my son and you approached near enough to the colt to tamper with his trappings. How do you think the thorns came to be there?"

"Redfeather must have slipped them in when tightening the girth," stated Dick without hesitating. "They were not there when *he* rode—that is clear."

25

"*Did* you put the thorns there?" asked Arrowhead, eyeing his son doubtfully.

"No, Father," answered Redfeather, trying to look as innocent as a new-born lamb. "It is a trick of the White Boy to get another contest. When he got back to his teepee he placed thorns in the blanket—and then told the squaw to feel. The White captives have many thorn twigs in their teepee."

"How do you know?" asked Arrowhead darkly.

"Let Eagle Eye explain," said Redfeather, motioning to the waiting youth.

Eagle Eye stepped forward and spoke: "It is true, O' Chief. The small boy, Ton-ie, collects butterflies and moths and kills them with sharp thorns. He has often shown them to me. *We* do not hoard such babyish rubbish," he patted his chest boastfully. "We collect scalps."

Disgusted, Dick listened to a plot which made him gasp with hot anger, as one by one Redfeather's chums stepped forward and with hand on heart gave their evidence. The way they explained about Tony's specimens, and how Dick had been seen the previous day among the thorn bushes (he'd been breaking some off for his little brother) made Arrowhead look angrily at Dick. [Most dangerous when calm, the Chief waved the boy away, and Dick knew that his fate was sealed.

"As you appear to like thorns," said Arrowhead, showing his teeth in a snarl, "a path of thorns shall be placed for you to-morrow and you'll run the

26

gauntlet before the whole tribe—after which you'll die spread-eagled on the ants' nest. Maybe when a horde of these little biters eat into your flesh, you'll remember—*thorns*."

With these dread words ringing in his ears, Dick walked back to his own wigwam.

CHAPTER IV

NIGHT IN THE FOREST

To May and Tony he made light of the interview, but told Gran the truth. She was horrified and clutched him to her bosom. Although a flinty old soul she had mothered the three White children for a year and really was as fond of them as they were of her.

"Then you must run away—at once, Deek," she announced.

Warner shook his head. "No, Gran, I know what would happen if I did—you would have to run the gauntlet in my place for allowing me to escape: that is the Indian law."

The squaw looked glum, then with a crafty gleam in her eyes and running a finger along her curved nose she said, "But not if I were tied up and found helpless in the morning."

May seized upon the idea at once and said they must prepare to escape.

"But," Dick objected, "really, Gran, we can't leave you all night trussed up."

The squaw grinned. "And I don't intend to be, Deekie. I'll manage my part—you get ready—now. During the hours of darkness you can be far away, through the forest and out on the prairie where you must hide by day in the long grass. Arrowhead will surely send his Braves to recapture you, so you must have the eyes of the hawk, the cunning of the wolverine. Leave everything except two blankets, one for you and Tony and one for Blossom, and food—and may the Great Spirit protect you."

Dick refused to go. "What will happen to you, Grannie?" he asked again. "At sunrise the Braves will come for me . . . and if I have gone . . ."

"I have a plan," replied the squaw, "hurry, hurry —you waste time."

"Tell me your plan."

"Dear, dear, what a stubborn boy you are! Very well: at sunrise when the Indian boy leaves the gourd of goat's milk outside he will hear me groan and look in and find me bound and gagged—now hurry."

Dick shook his head. "How could you bind and gag yourself so well as to deceive Arrowhead's Braves?"

Gran made a gesture of despair. "Just before the milk boy comes I'll get my married daughter Malva to come and do it. Am I a papoose to be questioned so?"

"Very well," Dick agreed; and so for a time the three children became busy, looking out their belongings, and what a pile they had, enough to stock a bazaar: bead and claw necklaces, bracelets, clothes of deerskin, hand-woven scarves, Tony's collection of butterflies and beetles. With a groan they threw them back into their baskets and selected necessaries:

29

Dick's bow and quiver of arrows, a spear for May, their strongest clothes of deerskin for the cold nights, a flint and steel, blankets and food and a goatskin filled with water. Even then the pile looked mountainous.

"It is time we put out the fire," said Gran, "or someone will become suspicious."

Dick went to the flap and looked out. The camp was in darkness and silent, every one asleep except the sentries. From the forest came the white owl's call *Choo-woo-a*! and the bark of a timber wolf. It needed courage to face those dark glades at midnight: prowling wild beasts and snakes in the grass, and sharp-eyed savage men on watch. Dick felt a weight like a stone on his heart. Should he leave May and Tony? No, they would suffer in his place.

When at last all three were ready, they looked so like tinkers going to a fair that Gran smiled, rather wanly. "You'll never go far with that load," she whispered. "Whatever is the matter with my little chick? He's grown fat suddenly."

Tony blushed and tried to pull away, but Dick grabbed him and unloaded from his waistline such an astonishing amount of wooden toys, beads, pressed flowers, pine-cone gollywogs and what not that all laughed.

Tony was allowed to keep a few small toys and then the three captives said goodbye to Gran and slipped silently into the night.

Danger was present even from the first moment.

Redskins are light sleepers, and three small shadows creeping into the forest at night might arouse suspicion. The night was cloudy, but there was sufficient light for sharp Indian eyes.

"Mind where you step," whispered Dick, "'ware tent-pegs and sleeping dogs. We'll go singly once we are clear of the wigwams and meet at the forest track."

During their captivity the three had learned some of the Indian habits and moved through the long lines of teepees with no sound except a sish-h of dead grass. There was now an open space between village and forest, and across it sped Tony with May close behind. Dick soon followed and the three struck into the dark forest.

The children knew where the sentries were posted and kept clear of the forest tracks. The deeper they penetrated into the forest, the thinner was the undergrowth until only a soft carpet of pine needles remained. Progress was at a snail pace; darkness seemed to flap in their faces like an invisible curtain; only at times could they get a glimpse of sky. Around them the night life of the forest went on: scutterings of wild creatures, the shuffle of a disturbed rabbit; in the branches a coon awoke and popped out of a hole; a sly lynx trailed them for a long way, and once they halted in affright as a bear reared up from a thicket and growled so savagely that Dick fitted an arrow to his bow expecting attack.

"We are past the last sentry now," he announced after a further long walk.

"Where are we making for?" asked May.

"The Pawnees will imagine we are working east—toward the White Settlement, so for a time we'll move north. When we are clear of the forest I can get direction from the stars, if the sky clears, but for the present we must steer by what wind there is, not much among the trees. Did you notice wind direction as we entered the forest, sister?" he tested her woodcraft.

"Rather—on the right cheek, and I keep checking it with a wet finger."

"Good for you," chuckled her brother. "I used to think I was clever at woodcraft until I became a Pawnee—we'll have rain before morning: yesterday

I saw several moles leaving their runs for higher ground. Our old Medicine Humbug will be in high glee. For weeks he's been asking his totem pole to send rain and there'll be a thunderstorm to-morrow."

"Which will make our trail easier to follow," said May.

"In the muddy parts . . . yes, but rain makes the trodden grass spring up again. The rain may save us yet."

"Let us hope so. Those Braves could see a thunder-fly a mile away. Don't they bite." She slapped a cheek. "Anyway, we'll hope for the best."

As it was late summer, dawn came early and a thin mist filled the forest aisles. The runaways were cold and weary, especially seven-year-old Tony, but Dick urged them on, until, where the trees began to thin out, he called a halt.

"Now we'll rest and have breakfast. We are practically out on the prairie now. Tony—get out the meat and bread while May and I have a scout around."

They had not far to go to the forest edge and gazed on a scene which opened their tired eyes: instead of the grassy prairie they expected to see was a row of Indian wigwams not two hundred yards away.

"From frying pan to fire," Dick choked out, staring wide eyed at the backs of the teepees showing clearer each moment through the tissue-paper mist. "We've run into a camp of strange Indians. We must be off——"

May clutched his arm and turned her frightened face to his.

"Dick! Oh, Dick!" she almost sobbed. "Don't you understand? Look!"

"God help us, yes," he groaned. "We've tired ourselves for nothing. The wind changed during the night and we've walked in a circle—we're back at Arrowhead's encampment."

This was a blow which shook them to the heart. Now that the mist was gone, the well-known totems on the wigwams were plain: the deer, the owl, Arrowhead's, their own with poor old Gran pretending to be bound and gagged. As yet the camp slept, but in an hour's time the milk boy would make a stir.

Really afraid, they ran back to Tony who saw by their expression that something terrible had happened. As it was impossible to hide the truth they told him.

"If we return to the wigwam no one will know we ran away," suggested Dick. "Shall we?"

For a moment or two May was too stunned to speak, but her brain was busy. It was a way out, safety for two of them, but death for her brother. Any instant now the camp might be roused and a search begun.

"No," she decided firmly.

"That's brave of you, sister," said Dick, "but all is not lost yet. We must hide and hope for the best."

"Where?"

"In our hollow basswood tree. Oh! what bad luck —two or three glimpses of the stars would have saved us that tiring night walk. Come along, Tony."

The huge basswood tree had been blasted by lightning many years before and ants had eaten out the heart until only a shell remained. It was just outside the Indian burial-ground, but being sensible children they had no fear of the graves over the low wall; it was, however, a fearsome place to the natives both young and old and consequently shunned. The Warners had made a playhouse inside the tree which was large enough to hold them all.

"We'll be all right in here," said Dick as he replaced the cunningly fitting piece of bark serving as a door. "There's going to be a storm, so that, except for the Braves sent out to fetch us back, none of the tribe will leave the teepees." He yawned, then grinned. "Anyway, I'm tired. I vote we have a meal and then we'll sleep snug as coons, because if we are still at liberty to-night, we've a long, long trail."

CHAPTER V

A FORTUNATE MISTAKE AFTER ALL

WHAT happened in the Pawnee camp the children never knew—they slept the sleep of exhaustion. In point of fact their error saved them. Having had several hours' start no one imagined they would be near camp. At daybreak Gran was found gagged and bound, and a hubbub arose in very truth. Gran acted well and spoke truly that the three Palefaces had been gone since midnight and must be far away. Arrowhead was wild as a trapped fox and sent Big Owl and the Braves and young men on the trail. But the Palefaces had a friend in Big Owl, and some of the Indians did not want to recapture the White Papooses, knowing they would surely die. Alone of the searchers Redfeather hunted with any keenness, but even he had to obey Big Owl who sent him and his mates on horseback through the forest to search the prairie away to the east, and in the late afternoon they came loping back—without prisoners.

Meanwhile, not a quarter mile away, the three runaways slept peacefully while thunder crackled and lightning blazed across the tree-tops and rain poured down in sheets. Only once did they come near to being recaptured and that was toward sunset, when Redfeather, returning from giving Mousie exercise, saw suspicious tracks, though almost obliterated by the storm, leading westward towards the cemetery, but the tracks vanished before he had gone a hundred yards. Rather fearfully he crept as far as the dead basswood tree and sheltered under the branches.

Dick almost betrayed himself. Awakening at dusk he rose and had a shock when he stared out through the crack in the bark and saw a copper-coloured shoulder within hand reach.

"Redfeather!" thought Dick, glancing down to where May still lay beside Tony. A movement, a word muttered in sleep and all would be lost.

Warner drew his knife determined to fight for liberty. The sight of Redfeather's shoulder so near enraged him; one downward thrust to the heart and the Chief's son would fall like a dropped sack; but Dick could not do it; in fair fight maybe—a treacherous attack—no.

Redfeather was thinking out how far the runaways could have travelled since midnight. That Paleface boy was a sly one to slip through the sentries and vanish. Redfeather would have another search in the morning and if he came up with the Paleface Dogs he'd scalp them and make excuse that they'd resisted, and Arrowhead would be pleased. Maybe it would mean another three honour feathers. Redfeather frowned as he recalled how his father, although undoubtedly angry, had seemed just a little amused when he heard that the Paleface Boy had

37

beaten the whole Pawnee tribe after all. Old Squaw Otter had been under suspicion, but was tied and gagged by someone who knew how to do it: Big Owl had said so, being first to see her after the milk boy had given the alarm. It was a wonder the squaw was alive. The Paleface had pounced on her while she slept (so Gran had said) and knocked her almost senseless—to prove it there was a bluish-green bruise mark—painted on with dyes by her daughter Malva— under the white hair near the forehead, and when Gran recovered she found herself bound and gagged. Redfeather did not like the way some of the squaws and warriors laughed at him, especially Squaw Otter's cronies, and even Big Owl—but he was second chief and above suspicion. . . .

The storm, too, occupied Redfeather's attention.

He was secretly afraid of the flashing thunder god and when a stricken tree fell not far away in the forest, he made a dash for his teepee.

Of a sudden Dick saw the crack in the bark lighten, and peering out saw Redfeather sprinting for the Indian village.

When May and Tony awoke, Dick said nothing about their narrow escape.

38

Now was the real testing time. They had a meal and prepared for the trail.

"Stay there," whispered Dick, "while I see if all is clear."

"*Do* be careful," warned May. "And don't be long."

It was quite dark when he stepped from the hiding-place and crawled to the forest edge. The storm had passed away, leaving a clear sky. He could see the dark triangles of teepees and several fires. Dick was about to crawl back, when a dark object away to the right caught his eye and he realised that it was a horse picketed with a long rope. Dick's heart bounded with a sudden hope and longing as the animal, disturbed, raised his head and revealed—Mousie. Redfeather had been too lazy to return him to the horse lines down in the lush grass by the river, instead merely ramming in the picketing pin when clear of the village.

Warner came to a quick decision. He had been cheated of Mousie—now was his chance. Approaching cautiously, he gave his usual horse talk, "Hoh-hoh!" in a deep voice, "Shuh-shuh," and hissing his low grasshopper twitter hoping that the colt would not be so delighted as to whinny.

Mousie was not too pleased. His last encounter with the human he now smelt was connected in his mind with stabs along the spine, but there were pleasant memories, too, of caresses and chunks of sweet food and tender hands.

Dick was taking a great risk, but his mind was made up. Tony was only seven and would soon tire; with Mousie's help they could make better speed. Dick slipped his hand along the head-rope down to the picketing pin and pulled it up, then led the colt gently away back to the hollow tree.

May and Tony stared when they saw the colt, and silently helped Dick to fasten the blankets to Mousie's back.

"Now, Tony," he whispered, "up you go—no thorns this time (a chuckle) and keep an eye open for branches or you'll find yourself slipping over his tail. I guess Mousie won't feel your weight more than a—um—mouse," which proved true, for beyond a quiver of flank muscles, he stood quiet until Dick chirruped him on.

Now their eyes were accustomed to the darkness they made good progress, striking deep into the forest and away from the sentries, but soon Dick felt a strong suspicion that they were being trailed: he had heard faint rustlings and the crackle of twigs. In the first open space he checked the colt and fitted an arrow to his bow, his eyes on the opening in the bushes through which they had come.

"Hist!" he warned, pulling the bowstring taut, "here it comes. Oh!—it's only a wolf. I won't shoot it."

Slackening his bow he ran towards the beast, waving his arms, and then stopped dead in his tracks as the animal, instead of turning tail, gave a low joyous wuff! and pranced around him.

The three stood laughing softly as their pet rolled on his back, showing evident pleasure at finding them.

"Now if that doesn't take the bun," said Dick. "However has he managed it? Go back!"

"He's a clever dog," said Tony delightedly. "You see how well I've trained him."

"Then you tell him to *go back*, Master Boaster," said Dick.

"Oh, can't he come with us?" begged the little fellow.

"No," said Dick firmly. "He'd be no use and would be sure to wuff at the wrong time."

"You don't care—now you've got Mousie," Tony pouted, near to tears. "You are a selfish——"

"Hush!" warned the sister. "This is no time to quarrel. We are not very far from the village. Speak in a whisper. Why not let Wolfie come with us, Dick?"

"Because Wolf's an Indian dog and only half trained and not very affectionate either. I could never make any sense of him."

"Nor I," sighed May, "but Tony likes him."

"We can't risk our lives for Tony's fancies," said Dick. "Mousie is useful—but a dog is not. He's made us waste valuable time already. Go back!" he ordered, threatening the animal with the unstrung bow.

Wolf winced and retreated—but not far. Dick chased him well into the bushes and then came back, muttering angrily, and lifting Tony on to the colt's back, they moved on.

But before five minutes had passed, a dark shape came loping after them and the children made no further attempt to shoo him away. Two of them were pleased to have him, and Dick wouldn't have minded if Wolf had been properly trained.

CHAPTER VI

GOOD LUCK—OR BAD?

A DAY had passed and the three fugitives were well away now, out of the forest area and surrounded by prairie. The going had been good; turn and turn about on Mousie; even Dick took a short ride when tired, but mostly Tony sat aloft with the blankets and food.

Really the runaways were in a desperate situation although they did not know it. Riverside Ranch was hundreds of miles away and all around them were savage Indians of the plains. Here and there a copse reared a green head like an island, with a pale blue ribbon of hills on the horizon towards which the fugitives were making.

Although enjoying their liberty, the two elder children kept a sharp eye roving over the scented prairie. It was fear of recapture which made Dick begin teaching Mousie his tricks. Each time they rested for refreshments he taught the colt to kneel at a tap on the forelegs and the command, "Die!"

Great fun! making him understand, and May and Tony roared with laughter when Dick 'died' himself to show the animal what was expected. By now, from kindness and numerous licks at chunks of maple sugar, he had lost all fear of the little humans, and when he learnt that every time he knelt meant a lick at something nice, they had some trouble in keeping him upright; and it was not long before his trick was needed.

May was first to sight the ant-size dots moving swiftly towards them. "Look, Dick!" she called out. "Either bison or Indians."

The dots were galloping Sioux who also had seen the tiny specks and meant to find out what they were.

"Die!" commanded Dick quickly, holding a slab of sugar to Mousie's nose, and down into the long grass he went. Dick spread a coloured blanket over him and sprinkled large convolvulus leaves and flowers on top; then wriggled under the blanket and stroked the colt's muzzle and let him lick the sugar. A few yards away May, and Tony cuddling the dog, lay snug as partridges completely hidden by feathery grass and white flowers as large as bugles. With ears to earth they were aware of the Redskins' approach.

Thump-thumpa-thump! sounded the galloping hoofs, with now and then a shrill cry from the Sioux Braves hoping to scare the 'game.'

Peeping from a clump of prairie sunflowers, May saw a painted feathered savage mounted on a mustang dash past, but among so many wild geraniums and white convolvulus, the flower-covered blanket was unnoticed and as the pounding of hoofs died away all breathed more freely.

"Whew-w-w!" whistled Dick. "If we hadn't

taught you that trick, Chummy, we'd have been caught again and I've had enough of Indian life."

"And I," May echoed, rising and dusting pollen from her brown dress. "Old Gran was a decent old soul, really, but I prefer Riverside Ranch. The apples, pears and peaches will be about ready when we arrive."

"Hurrah!" cried Tony, admiring a big captive butterfly. He was making a collection for Mam, killing them painlessly and swiftly with a thorn and pressing them between leaves.

By now the three runaways were merry again, especially at thought of their Ranch and were constantly talking of what they would do when they arrived.

"Why, Tony, Mam will think you're an Indian if you don't scrub some of that sunburn off," Dick joked when the little boy showed a dislike for plunging into the streams they passed. Dick and May could swim like salmon, but Tony, having once been thrown into a deep pool by a bullying Brave, had not overcome his nervousness.

Tired out, the children reached the wooded foothills just as the sun was sinking into the prairie grass, and while searching for a likely camping place for the night, Dick made a discovery.

"I've found a track, sister," he called out excitedly. "Come and see what you make of it."

Bent double, May took a long look at the ground while Dick stood smiling near by. From the Indians they had learned much not contained in books.

"A Paleface lives not far away," said May, "but he is not at home and sometimes has visitors: he is tall and smokes Indian tobacco, using matches, lucky man; slightly lame in his right leg . . . er . . ."

"All right," chuckled Dick, "that's easy: you guessed his height by the length of his stride; there's a dottle of tobacco from his pipe; he's not at home because the tracks of his Mexican boots—note the small heel—are old, not sharp edged, and his lameness shows in the lighter impression of his right foot—perhaps he hurt himself with his axe—he's not a woodsman or he wouldn't use a blunt axe. . . ."

"All right," echoed May, "that's easy—the cuts in that log show the state of his axe edge, but *Indians* use stolen axes and I've seen conceited young Braves wear boots. Now, Dickie Hawkeye, how do I know he's a White man?"

"His horse is shod," Dick answered, pointing to a hoof mark.

"Not bad. How about this?" She held out an empty ·45 revolver cartridge. "You missed that clue, Mr. Mole-eye: it was under one of those chips. I wonder where he keeps his donkey?" indicating a small hoof mark. "Anyway—Hi-o! Up the trail we go and we'll have shelter for to-night in his cabin." The tree stumps proved he had built a log cabin.

The three Warner children stared across a clearing not far up the track; in the centre was a small log shack, and Indian-wise the brains of all three were busy—Tony was learning woodcraft from his elders.

"An *old* shack," said Tony proudly. "The log ends are weathered and mossy, but that shed behind is fairly new—the cut ends are white."

Dick patted him. "Good boy, and I guess Mousie will like being there."

"You're only guessing," said Tony; "that's not fair. You can't see any hay or corn."

"The tin chimney gives the clue," said May, smacking her lips. "That shed is too small to live in, so it must be used for boiling maple sugar; besides, there's a shallow cooling tin just outside. Come on. It's growing dark. Mr. Hermit has not been home for days." A mass of spider webs across the door had given her the clue.

"Good evening," Dick called out, pulling the

47

latch-string and pushing open the door. "May we come in?"

Of course they knew the place was vacant and entered at once. Doors were seldom locked out in the wilds and it was customary for wayfarers to make use of huts. In high glee May flitted from box to box exclaiming, "Oh! Good—flour, oatmeal, dried peas, beans, sugar for Mousie——"

From habit she prowled carefully around and when Dick returned after securing the colt in the smaller shed and feeding him with hay and corn, they compared clues.

"Queer, why a *young* man should live out here," said Dick, tossing a wide-brimmed hat back on to its high hook.

"It is," May answered. "*I* saw those fair hairs inside that hat; especially queer when he troubles to shave and keep his nails trimmed . . . is intelligent . . . kind hearted . . .?

Dick laughed. "Hold your donkey in, sister. You'll be telling me next which school he went to and the size of his boots. . . ."

"Size nine . . . school—Portland, Oregan."

"You'd better join Pinkerton's Detective Agency," smiled puzzled Dick, tickling his scalp. "About this kind heartedness?"

"A man who looks well after sick animals——" May got in rather a muddle, and both laughed. "Look at those bottles of horse physic and there's a book entitled *Animal Diseases* on that shelf. The

48

name of a school is written inside—not necessarily his, but most likely."

Dick took up the paper-backed book. "Um! His own name scratched out—I guessed as much." He walked round the cabin. "Use only dry wood for the fire, sister; we don't want to attract Mr. Bad Man's attention——"

May paused, matchbox in hand. "I was afraid so," she said quietly, so Tony could not hear. "Too many rifles, revolvers and ammunition hidden all over the hut. Too many expensive articles a hermit would not need, and obviously he is not a trapper."

"And too many saddles and bridles in the next hut, and worst of all—several branding irons," whispered Dick, "not to mention—*this*," holding up an object which made the girl shudder—a torn black silk mask.

"So now we have him placed," said Dick: "a smart young bandit kind to horses, but he might not be so kind to three penniless boarders." He eyed the stump of candle May had lighted. "Leave it. Here's a rug to cover the window, although I don't think he is anywhere near. I'll get the fire going while you prepare supper and then I'll have a scout outside."

CHAPTER VII

A DISTURBED NIGHT

DICK was a long time away and May knew what he was doing. She had not asked why he wanted a few empty tins and a length of rope. Dick did not intend being surprised and was fastening a booby trap across the track. When he returned he looked pleased.

"Dark as a dungeon outside," he said. "Those tin cans on a line will surprise the outlaw, if he's anywhere around. There are no other tracks to the shack. Now what's for supper? Hi-O! Smells good," lifting a pan lid and sniffing. "Cheers!—bunny stew."

"That's Wolfie's contribution to the feast," said May. "He brought it in just after you went out. Tony! What are you doing in that corner? Come and help me."

"I caught him," cried the little fellow, gleefully showing a closed fist from which peeped a mouse's tail. "There's a nest of young ones——".

"Gracious! Let it go," cried the sister in disgust. "You are always after live things."

Tony obeyed by letting the wee mouse jump on to her arm, making her squeal.

"Hey! Stop that," warned the elder boy; and

May understood instantly that they must make no noise.

Dick fetched another can of water from the spring at the back of the shack, while May stirred the cut-up rabbit and added dumplings of flour and water. While it was stewing she collected the ingredients for bannocks (scones) and pancakes. The former were only of dough made from flour and water and baked on a tin set on the hearth, and the mixture for pancakes—flour and quail eggs (similar to partridge) collected that day on the prairie. When the mixture was beaten up she put it on one side because the rabbit would take an hour to stew and pancakes must be cooked and eaten fresh from the pan. A huge tin of maple syrup was already on the table together with a plate of blueberries for dessert.

After a grand supper May inspected the two wooden bunks, and after clearing away spiders and dust, said they were fit to use.

"Come along, Tony boy, you've no need to wash or undress to-night. Into the top bunk you go, and leave room for me—Dick can have the lower one."

"Don't bother," said Dick, "I'm staying up to read this old magazine I found in the corner."

May nodded, knowing he meant to keep watch.

They were in a dangerous fix—far more to be dreaded than among Pawnees. That the shack was the hide-out of robbers was clear, and bad White man's cruelty is very different from Redskins'.

May listened while Tony said, "Our Father . . ."

then kissed him and lifted him into the bunk; and then, having washed the supper plates and pans, she climbed up herself, leaving the lower bunk for Dick if he should decide to use it.

All was now silent except for Mousie next door who still champed his fodder and snorted now and then, but not loud enough to cause any alarm.

May and Tony were soon asleep, and Dick, using the dog's stretched-out body as a footstool, yawned over his magazine. To keep awake he blew out the candle and went out for a prowl. In his tired state it was unwise to sit down on a log, with his back comfortable against a pine, but he yielded to temptation and was soon asleep—and dreaming—telling his parents of his adventures—and then (as Mousie snorted) his dream turned to the Ranch corral. Suddenly the cattle turned into sleigh horses with bells tinkling—ding-ding-tinkle-dong-PONG——

He awoke with thudding heart and jumped upright —not bells but his booby trap of tins—clang-clong— someone was coming up the trail—he must warn May and Tony.

With hardly a sound Dick raced back to the cabin and shook his sister into wakefulness. "Someone coming," he whispered. "You and Tony go outside —quick—and hide behind the sugar shed. Get your six-gun, May. Hurry! Quiet, Wolf!" to the growling dog which, with hair a-bristle, was facing the open door.

Dick was outside again in a flash and down the trail,

just in time to see a dark head and shoulders rise above a bush not five yards away.

"Who's there?" he called out, but instantly realised his error as with a WHOOF! of fury a huge grizzly bear sprang towards him.

The boy side-stepped as he pulled the trigger and the Wham! of the rifle-shot awoke the sleeping echoes of the forest. He felt the wind fan his cheek as a paw clawed at his head. Dodging another blow he took to his heels.

The forest was now rustling with wild things disturbed from sleep: flutterings of birds and bats; squirrels jumped to higher branches; a timber wolf prowling near Mousie went scuttering off with a spitting snarl. Outside the sugar shed Dick heard May trying to soothe the stamping colt and ran to her side.

"A grizzly!" he called out. "I had to fire or he'd have clawed me. Go back into the hut."

In the race for the shack the three children won by a hairsbreadth. Indeed Dick had to slam the door in the brute's face, and the heavy bar was hardly in place when CRASH! came its furious body against the woodwork. With thudding hearts the three stood in the glow of the fire listening to the sounds outside: first the scratching of claws on the logs, followed by a sniffing up and down the jamb; then came an angry growl and a barking sound as the dog came to do his bit.

"Did you close the door of the sugar shed?" asked Dick in great alarm.

"Yes, but it's only on the latch," May answered.

"Goodness!—that brute will have Mousie for a certainty——"

His words were clipped off by a crash of glass and down came the rug covering the window. Immediately the empty square framed a great black head looking in, wicked eyes red as rubies, teeth like ivory daggers; but Dick and May dare not fire for fear of hitting Tony. The table being farthest away from the door, he had scrambled upon it and so was right in the line of fire; indeed, had he reached out, he could have hit the bear on the nose.

"Lie flat, Tony!" Dick yelled, and so quick did he obey in his fright that he rolled clear off the table.

Tony's thud and two gunshots came together.

"We didn't get him," said Dick, as he hurried through the gunsmoke to the window and looked out, just in time to see Bruin sneaking up to the door of the sugar shed.

Dick's affection for Mousie made him forget all else and become reckless. It would be a terrible blow to lose the colt. A bear is not easy to kill in daylight; in almost pitch darkness he presents only a vague target. He was already wounded in two places —sufficient to make him savage—but not in vital spots. Dropping his rifle outside the window he climbed through and, recovering his weapon, ran towards where the bear had disappeared round the end of the shed. By this time Bruin had patted down the door of the sugar shed and as Dick turned the corner he caught only a glimpse of his stubby tail as he crept inside to enjoy the horse meal he had smelt.

But, in spite of his name, Mousie was no mouse. Instinctively he had turned his tail to the danger point and as the grizzly bear reared to strike with curved claws, Mousie lashed out with all the force of his strong hoofs.

The blow caught Bruin under the jaw, throwing him off his balance, so that he lay sprawling in the doorway when Dick arrived. Quick as a wink Dick poked his rifle muzzle into the brute's ear and pulled the trigger. Bruin emitted a short whoff! and lay still.

"Is it dead?" came May's voice from the rear.

Dick laughed. "I could hardly miss at that range.

Dead as mutton, he is. Help me to pull him away from the doorway and we'll have Mousie out."

May sighed. "We've no luck, Dick; just when we find a comfortable home—we have to move. If the owner of this hut is anywhere around he will come tearing back. What time do you think it is?"

"No idea. I fell asleep."

Dick had slept longer than he thought, for, as they collected their belongings, the darkness changed to grey—it was morning.

"We'll have a cold breakfast," said Dick, "and leave the cabin as tidy as we possibly can. I'm sorry about the window, but we can nail boards across in case Mr. Bandit doesn't come back for a few days. Where's Tony?"

They found him outside flourishing a bowie-knife over the bear.

"No need to be afraid, kid," said Dick, "it is quite dead."

"I know—I'm going to skin it——"

"Don't be silly," said May, "it would take you a week. Give me that knife."

"I want the fur for a present for Mam," said Tony, turning obstinate.

"All right," said Dick, "we'll leave you here . . . now, now, no whimpering! Even if we got the skin off we've not enough salt and alum to cure it. We'll leave Bruin in exchange for a couple of revolvers and cartridges——"

"No, no, Dick," May objected, rather half-
56

heartedly, knowing how useful a revolver would be, "fair play. That would be almost like stealing."

"*Borrowing*," Dick corrected. "I know what we'll do—leave an I OWE YOU, and I'm sure Dad would send back what we had borrowed."

May agreed. "Come inside and we'll write a note and pin it on the table."

She found a stub of pencil and a strip of wrapping paper and wrote:

DEAR SIR,

We are in a fix and have a long way to go, so have taken the following things for which we leave an I.O.U. Our Father will send them back and pay you well.

Thank you, and hope you won't mind.

DICK, MAY and TONY WARNER,
RIVERSIDE RANCH,
NEBRASKA, U.S.A.

Things taken:—

2 revolvers, belts and cartridges.   1 saddle and bridle.
1 tin dish.   1 pot of dripping.   1 axe.

"I think that's fair enough," Dick remarked, "and as make-weight," he joked, "we'll leave Tony's bag of tricks."

"No, you won't," said Tony, grabbing his bag of specimens and thumping Dick's back. "These pressed butterflies and things are for Mam and Dad."

"Cheer up, kid, I'm only funning," laughed Dick, ruffling Tony's curls. "Now we'll have breakfast and hit the trail."

CHAPTER VIII

A CHEERFUL CAMP

"IF we go on at this rate," chuckled Dick an hour later as they set off eastwards, "we'll need a wagon. We start off with bread, pemmican and water and now look at Mousie."

He was indeed a sight and appeared none too pleased at being loaded like a pack mule: blankets, food, a metal water-canteen they had taken in exchange for the goatskin, all piled high on the new saddle; there was a bridle and bit too, but fortunately for the colt's peace of mind, he knew not their purpose. When, after another hour, Tony was lifted on to the pile, Mousie halted and turned a surprised eye on his master.

"I'm sorry, Mousie," Dick whispered into his ear as he fed him with sugar, "but we're in a fix and you must do your share. I hope you had a good feed of hay and corn, chum, because, if I guess aright, we have a tough journey ahead."

The children had heard the Pawnees speak of the stony waste-land known as the chaparral with the desert beyond and already the lush prairie grass was thinning out into sandy patches on which grew sharp-thorned cactus. The sweet scent of flowers had changed to an odour of sage and creosote bushes. To avoid this desert was impossible: it stretched for miles right across their path and to go around would add hundreds of miles to the journey.

By now the elder children had given up all pretence and faced facts bravely, and all whistled and sang as they tramped along.

The old song *When Johnny Comes Marching Home Again* (slightly altered) made Tony feel important:

When Tony comes marching home again—Hurrah! Hurrah!
  We'll give him a hearty welcome then, Hurrah! Hurrah!
The men will cheer, the boys will shout,
  The 'punchers they will all turn out;

CHORUS: *And we'll all feel gay when Tony comes marching home,*
  And we'll all feel gay when Tony comes marching home.

The old Ranch bell will peal with joy—Hurrah! Hurrah!
  To welcome home our darling boy, Hurrah! Hurrah!
The stable lads and cowboys say,
  With dollars they will strew the way;

CHORUS: *And we'll all feel gay when Dickie comes marching home,*
  And we'll all feel gay when Dickie comes marching home.

Get ready for the Ju-bi-lee—Hurrah! Hurrah!
  We'll give the heroes three times three—Hurrah! Hurrah!
The laurel-wreath is ready now,
  To place upon each sunburnt brow;

59

CHORUS: *And we'll all feel gay when the trio comes marching*
home,
And we'll all feel gay when the trio comes marching
home.

Let love and friendship on that day—Hurrah! Hurrah!
Their choicest treasures give to May—Hurrah! Hurrah!
And let each one perform his part,
To fill with joy our sister's heart;

CHORUS: *And we'll all feel gay when our May comes marching*
home,
And we'll all feel gay when our May comes marching
home.

Each step was towards home and no better spur
could be wished for. Somewhere below where the
sun was shining stood Riverside Ranch and already
their minds were picturing what the reunion would be.

"Won't Mam and Dad stare when we come riding
up," said Tony from his high perch on the Mexican
saddle. "This is easier riding, Dickie Bird, but I'd
like a run with Wolfie."

Dick lifted him down and decided to make camp
to think things out. Already the water-container
was almost empty and there would be no streams or
water holes out in the chaparral. Judging by the
height of the sun the time was late afternoon; it
would be safer to tackle the desert at sunrise.

"We'll camp for the night in that distant copse,"
said Dick. "There is sure to be water. Your turn to
ride, May. Up you go."

The small wood made a good hiding-place and

provided all they wanted for a camp, and soon all three were busy. Mousie was picketed on a patch of grass while Tony went scouting for water and soon called out that he had found a spring. With the axe Dick cut a pile of fir branches to form springy mattresses on which to spread the blankets. He then collected dry twigs of beech and maple for a fire while May prepared a meal; then Dick went to find

Tony, found that the water was drinkable and returned for Mousie.

May also had been busy. The five birds, resembling partridges, shot by arrows the previous day, were plucked and cleaned and stuffed with nuts and squashed ripe rowan berries. She then skewered the quail on to a thin hickory twig so that only an occasional turn of the twig was necessary to brown them all round, with the tin dish beneath to catch some of the dripping.

"Do you think the smoke from our fire can be seen?" asked May, handing a luscious-looking bird to Dick and then a smaller one to Tony.

"Not with dry twigs," Dick answered. "We are well hidden in the wood and what smoke filters through the tree tops couldn't be seen two hundred yards away. While the fire is alight, sister, bake a few more cakes. There'll be no wood beyond the chaparral. I wish we had a bigger water-container because we couldn't last many days on cactus fruit."

"Why, Dick," exclaimed May, "you aren't expecting being *days* in the desert?"

"I hope not. . . . Anyway, we mustn't get scared."

The night passed without any alarm and at grey dawn after a breakfast of cold meat, bread and water, they set off singing merrily and leaving the future to fate.

As the sun mounted higher, the heat began to rise in waves from the stones and sand, until by noon their mouths were like sandpaper. Song and whistle had long since died away on parched lips and for a time none of them had spoken. On—on—on they plodded, feet now ploughing through the sand, leg muscles already aching. Behind them, almost treading on his lolling tongue, padded the dog, every now and then looking up pleadingly to Dick as though asking: Wherever *are* you taking us?

At last they were forced to halt. Dick wiped the sweat from his eyes and grinned, and after licking his lips was just able to gasp out the words, "Camp . . . here."

First a drink from the canteen and, although warm, never was water better appreciated, loosening tongues and washing sand from parched throats and bringing on a measure of hunger. Off came Mousie's pack and with bow and spear as supports a shady tent of sorts was erected with two blankets.

The wayfarers squatted in the shade to eat.

"Do you think we'll have much of this?" asked May.

"I don't know," Dick answered truthfully. "What else could we have done? We dare not delay for fear of Arrowhead's warriors trailing us and we should have had to tackle the desert some time—it lies right across our path. Better try while we are fairly fresh."

May remained silent, not enjoying the situation, and would have liked to suggest going back while they had a chance. The heat seemed to have sapped her strength already and at most there was water for only two days. The white skeletons of animals they had passed were dreadful reminders of their peril; but she kept her fears to herself, mostly for Tony's sake.

Refreshed but not rested they rose and loaded Mousie again and struck doggedly into the fiery sand . . . with Tony riding.

CHAPTER IX

THE DESERT OF DEATH

FIVE hours passed with never a word and by now poor Tony had to be held on his perch by Dick's strong arm. Jog—jog—the little lad had the true grit of the Pioneers in his blood. Not a whimper or grumble came from him, as he knew how hard it was for his elders to keep plodding on—left right, left right, with feet like leaden weights. . . .

They halted as the sun drooped towards the west and now shone on their backs. Dick was too good a scout to go in a circle with the sun telling him the time and direction. For long hours now the hills they had left had sunk below the horizon and nothing remained but sand and sky. Only once had they seen signs of life—distant moving objects which might have been either Indians or wild mustangs.

Again the blanket tent was rigged and precious water doled out, followed by what food they could swallow—very little indeed. Mousie and Wolfie had their share, too, and it was heart-rending to see the way they licked up every drop and nudged Dick for more. When offered a handful of hay Mousie snorted and stood with hanging head, crunching his sugar languidly.

"He seems uneasy," said May, watching the

colt pawing the sand and rolling his bloodshot eyes.

"And so am I," Dick smiled wanly. "Look at Tony there. Thank the Good God he can sleep and forget. I don't like the outlook, May."

"Nor I. We'll never do it."

Dick's lips made a firm line. "We *must*, May. We have water for another day——"

"And then . . .?"

For answer Dick pointed to a heap of bones now tinted pink in the setting sun.

"How about going back?" May suggested. "We could just manage to get back to the little wood."

For a time the sister and brother sat worrying over that all-important problem and at last both came to the same conclusion: they would go back. It was a wise decision. Better to face bandits or be prisoners among Pawnees than become whitened skeletons. They could now see that their preparations had been too hurried.

But neither had a chance to voice their decision because Mousie decided for them. That the colt would run away never entered their thoughts—but he did, taking no notice of Dick's shrill whistle which awoke Tony.

Absolutely stunned, the three stood and watched the truant grow smaller and smaller, making straight westward towards the sweet pasture he remembered.

Tony slumped down again under the tent and while rubbing his eyes as though sleepy, brushed away a

E

tear, and, aware of it, both Dick and May felt a twinge of guilt.

So, filled with dismay, they sat until twilight brought coolness and . . . something else. . . at first black specks high aloft which grew in size, until with a fluttering of wings a dozen cruel-beaked vultures settled on the sand around them and began to preen their scraggy neck feathers—waiting for the feast.

The sun sank in blood-red streaks and soon the waning moon silvered the desert sand.

Something soft touching his face caused Dick's dream to switch over to Mousie—a vivid dream indeed—the same velvet muzzle, the warm breath; a whinnying sound made him open his eyes, but he imagined he still slept, although it was morning. Looking down at him were Mousie's eyes, with behind him a second dark shape—a black horse.

Dick sprang to his feet with a yell which woke Tony and May.

"Hurrah! Hurrah!" they heard Dick cry. "Good old Mousie! Wake up, sleepers. We are saved—Mousie has come back."

May knuckled her eyes at sight of the second animal.

"Am I squinting," she laughed, "or is it—Mousie's mother?"

Dick pointed to the white flash on the mare's forehead, the white fetlocks and a patch of white on her back.

"She looks as though she's wearing socks," cried Tony, "but she's not Mousie's mother."

"Too old," was Dick's opinion.

"It's a miracle," said May. "Where has she come from?"

"At a guess," said the elder boy, "I suggest Mousie found that drove of wild horses we saw yesterday and imagined that this magpie mare was his relation."

"But look! She has a bridle on!"

"Sometimes, sister, ranch horses run away when they scent a herd. That's what has happened . . . and not long ago either, because Magpie is not very shy. Give her a crunch of sugar and grab her reins while I coax Mousie."

67

But the colt needed no tempting. Whether his horse sense had sent him off for help, or whether he had intended running away, was a secret he alone knew. Perhaps the sight of the black-and-white mare running with the herd had reminded him of the Indian camp and his soot-coloured mother. For a time he had run beside her until he could steer her clear, and then had seized her trailing bridle and struck back into the desert. No one would ever know except the good angel who looks after lost children. . . .

CHAPTER X

NO FOOD—NO WATER—NO HOPE

THE outlook for the Warner children was now more hopeful, and they decided not to go back. During his truancy Mousie had found water and was refreshed already. He whinnied with delight when May put Tony on his back and sprang up behind him while Dick mounted Mousie's present, the new Magpie.

"Tally ho! Away we go!" cried Dick Warner, butting his bare heels into the mare's fat ribs. "Luck is with us. Look! . . . those birds know we are saved," he waved his revolver at the vultures, and watched them take wing one by one and disappear into the sun-baked sky. Although Dick pulled on the head-rope with all his might, the colt seemed determined to swerve north-east instead of east, so that at the first halt Dick decided to try him with the bit in his mouth. He coated the steel with maple sugar, and Mousie's laugh of delight was cut short when something hard was popped between his jaws and his ears slipped into straps. It was a tustle and Mousie danced a jig and shook his head and squealed as the steel rasped his tongue, but finding the sugary thing was in his mouth to stay, soon quietened down.

They now made better progress, but even the bit did not prevent Mousie from going where he pleased and when, four hours later, they struck rocky country and the colt halted at a gushing spring, Dick patted him for a cute fellow.

"We humans think we are clever," he said to May as she filled the water-canteen while Dick held the horses, "but we have much to learn from animals. Shall we rest or push on?"

"I'm going to take this chance and have a wash and brush up," she smiled, paddling into the pool. "Did you bring any soap, brother dear?"

"Sorry, sister, I forgot. Tony left it on the squaw's grand piano."

That made Tony laugh. "She hadn't a piano," he said, thumping his teasing brother, "but I'm sorry I left that bearskin——"

"See to your own bare skin," shouted May from behind a rock, "and get washed. The bath water's ready—nice and cool."

"I'll bathe if you promise to go back for that grizzly bearskin," he pouted, only in fun, but as Dick sprang for him with the intention of giving him a ducking, Tony jumped into the pool and was soon splashing around.

Looking refreshed May came out and held the horses while Dick pretended to catch minnows behind the rock. In the hot sun towels were not needed and he soon appeared dressed in his leather trousers.

"Now for some refreshments," he said, opening the bundle and throwing a strip of leathery-looking pemmican to Wolf, "and then Hi-o! for Riverside Ranch."

There was enough short grass round the spring to give Mousie a good feed, and prickly pears for the children, and they were soon off again.

They might have crossed the desert safely had not little Tony fallen sick. When they halted at sunset, and May, noting Tony's grey look even under his tan, asked him if he was all right, Tony admitted to "a bit of a headache."

"A touch of the sun," said Dick, stroking Tony's forehead as he lay in his sister's arms. "It was hot enough in the Pawnee camp, but this desert heat is awful—seems to rise in waves from the sand. I'd feel cooler in an oven. Can we do anything for him?"

71

"I don't know," said May. "Gran had some queer though useful medicines, but they don't grow on deserts. We'll try bathing his head with a wet rag. I'll see to him while you hobble the horses and get camp ready."

All that night poor Tony muttered in his sleep: about Gran and Redfeather, butterflies and frogs, the Ranch and a grizzly skin—all jumbled into nonsense. Nothing could be done for him, and the morning brought no change.

Dick looked glum. "We must really push on," he said. "Our food and water won't last very long."

It was the only hope. They did not know that many miles of desert still lay ahead, or would have given up in despair. By now the horses came muzzling for a drink and they must have their share; Wolf too. He was not a very lovable dog: too slinking and quiet—that was his half-wild nature—and while Dick and May were busy with little Tony, Wolf forgot what training he'd had and helped himself from the food package: pushing in his sharp wolf nose and gobbling all within reach, but always so slyly that neither Dick nor May guessed for a time.

At sunrise they saddled up and set off. Dick rode the old mare and had made a sling of a blanket where Tony could lie as though in a hammock, which he fastened on his back—when facing the sun— switching it over to the saddle horn towards sunset. Mousie carried May and the bundles.

On—on—on for two days, mostly at a walk, for all, even the beasts, were feeling the strain. In the cool of morning and at sunset, the animals' pace increased to a jog-trot lope, but always half hearted.

The water was now all gone, food too. Tony was a little better, though too weak to sit up for long. Far behind, like a black dot on a yellow tablecloth, trotted Wolfie with hanging tongue. The children were now too miserable to bother about him. None had spoken for many hours; tongues felt too big for their mouths. Only by a great effort of will power could they sit upright on their mounts. Dick's eyes were red-rimmed with gazing hopefully ahead, always expecting to see signs of a change in the landscape.

Actually they had accomplished a feat which would have tested the strength and courage of grown men; only children hardened by Redskin life could have done it.

The pace slackened to a walk . . . and then to a crawl . . . then the gallant horses halted of their own accord. When the children dismounted, both Mousie and Magpie flopped into a heap of panting flesh.

There's no need to say 'die' to Mousie, thought Dick. Poor brave fellow . . . and Magpie, too. We're finished, chums. No water, no food, no hope. You've done your best for us. . . .

From habit he put up the tent and the three sat close, hand in hand; and once more came the flapping of huge wings—the birds of death had come again.

Although the Warners had been kind to Wolf he

73

had little affection for them, except perhaps Tony whose special property he was. All that mattered to the Indian dog was to save his own life and for a time his keen sense of smell had told him that water lay ahead; and when darkness came on and the children slept he took a final smell around the empty food container and slunk silently away into the waste of desert sand.

After hours of silent plodding the sense of danger took away some of the dog's tiredness. The desert had changed again into the cactus and sage of the chaparral, among which lurked Wolf's enemies—coyotes. Fortunately the slight breeze was coming from them to him so that he sat on his haunches unnoticed, nose to wind and sniffed. The many new smells ahead were alarming, but he recognised a few —quite near there was a camp of humans, not Indians; also horses, cattle, burnt-out fires, meat and . . . *water*.

Crouching low to earth he crawled through the ring of coyotes and approached a cluster of strange objects large as teepees but with round tops. Wolf had never seen prairie schooners but knew they held men, and he advanced because, being now 'up wind,' his scent was being followed by coyotes. The cool scent of water was now overpowering and his quick ears had detected the gurgling of a spring. Like a shadow he crept under wheels into the drawn-up square of wagons and was soon lapping water joyously.

CHAPTER XI

ONLY JUST IN TIME

AT the first streak of daylight Wolf was soon disturbed by camp dogs nosing for scraps under the wagons. The yapping attracted the attention of Old Trapper Eli, one of the gold seekers, and at his call several rough-looking men jumped down from their covered wagons and formed a ring round the snarling dogs who kept at a safe distance from Wolf's bared fangs.

"That cur is Indian!" exclaimed Eli, "and by the look of that embroidered collar—Pawnee. Leave him to me."

Seizing his opportunity when Wolf was backing away from the threatening dogs, Eli rushed in and grabbed the collar. When the stranger was safely chained to a wagon wheel, the dogs were beaten off.

Wolf's arrival had caused great excitement in the camp. For days they had been on the watch for signs of Indians, and now here was proof.

"I know those Pawnee rogues to my sorrow," went on Trapper Eli. "I was once captured by Arrowhead's tribe and left my scalp in his wigwam. That cur didn't cross the Desert of Death alone. Oh, no! Look to your firearms, men, the Redskins are not far off."

The gold seekers were the advance party of hundreds of others all making for the desert in order to cross in safety. The magnet drawing them was GOLD, recently discovered at Placerville, California, nearly one thousand miles farther west. The precious metal had been found quite accidentally. A farmer had erected a water mill to grind his own corn and had turned the stream into a tail-race to get power to work the wheel. One evening when the mill stopped grinding he noticed that the bottom of the tail-race was covered with yellow specks. After weighing them and testing with acid he was jubilant: it was gold without a doubt.

The news spread eastwards like an epidemic and a Gold Rush started. Men of all types with their families left their occupations in order to Get Rich Quick and raced westwards with all speed, and Eli's wagons were well ahead.

"Be careful with the fires," he warned the women preparing breakfast. "Those Red fiends have eyes like vultures and I've seen a few around already. I'll warrant there's a deserted Indian camp not far away and this cur's been left behind. Three men come with me to scout."

He picked out an ex-cowboy, a Spanish cow-puncher and a young fellow who, judging by his scarlet tunic and yellow-striped breeches, was a deserter from the U.S. Army. They were, in fact, a mixed lot, rough as a file and differently dressed. The swarthy skins and speech of most of the women indicated 'foreigner'—banded together against the common danger—the desert and Red Men—but by no means friendly one to another. If the opportunity came each was capable of pilfering from his neighbour. That was why Jose Toldo, one of the Spaniards, decided to adopt Wolf, and before he went scouting, as ordered by Eli, dragged the scared dog up to his covered wagon where he tied him to a wheel.

"Oh, Jose!" exclaimed his stout wife Carlota. "Have we to live with that brute of a . . . what is it?"

"Indian cur . . . he's no beauty, but will keep those light-fingered hombres (fellows) from stealing my goods and it will be something for the bambino (child) to play with. I go on a scout now. Watch out, Carlota."

Without touching stirrups Jose sprang on to his mustang and galloped away.

After loping along for some time he suddenly pulled up sharp as an object caught his roving eye—a striped blanket flapping gently in the morning breeze. Jose stroked his dark moustache and showed white teeth in a grin of triumph. An Indian blanket . . . and stretched out beside it two horses, one grey, the other piebald; they looked dead, but Jose knew by the way the vultures kept at a distance that a spark of life remained.

Riding quickly up he stared dumb with astonishment at the unconscious forms of three children huddled near the blanket.

"Pawnee papooses!" he exclaimed.

Dismounting, he stooped and shook Dick Warner. "Wake up, boy! What are you doing out here? What! Another boy and a girl! You all look in a bad way...."

Although a rough man he had a soft place in his heart for children: had he not a lively boy in his wagon? Here was a lucky find: these three children had evidently lived with the Pawnees—their dress, the bow and arrows, the coloured blanket, the Indian spear. Jose knelt down and became busy, trying to revive the sleepers: water was dribbled between their lips, little hands were rubbed to restore circulation. He pummelled Dick and shook May, but they flopped back to the sand like sacks each time he lifted them.

May was the first to show signs of life, and looked afraid when, through half-closed eyelids, she saw a dark-faced man. A bandit, was her first thought . . . but a kind one. Her hot mouth was cooler now and throat wet where water had spilled over. With a groan she sat up and looked around. The stranger showed his teeth in a grin. "Good, good, my bonny bambino," he encouraged. "You were lost, eh? Lucky that Jose came, what? You not Pawnee children?"

May shook her head, being unable to speak. Instead she smiled, and leaning over pulled Tony nearer, making a sign for water by touching Tony's lips. Jose obeyed, and leaving the tin cup within her reach, carried his water-canteen to Dick who soon came round.

He stared, too, but realising that they had escaped death by the thickness of a sunbeam, grasped Jose's hand.

CHAPTER XII

THE GOLDEN ARMY

AN hour passed before either of the children could speak; Tony still lay unconscious.

"Thanks . . . kind friend," said Dick. "That was . . . a close thing."

"How did you find us?" asked May.

Jose jerked a thumb towards the rising sun and explained about Wolf.

"Good for the husky," cried Dick. "He's turned out to be useful after all."

Jose laughed. "I came to have scout round for Redskins," he explained. "No idea to find White children. Where do you live?"

"At Riverside Ranch, Nebraska," Dick answered.

Jose did not know it and said so.

"Are there many people with you?" asked May.

"Sure. Many caravans. In one are my wife and lovely baby boy . . . and a thief in camp. That is why I want dog . . . to keep guard, see?"

"How fortunate," said May. "We'll make you a present of Wolfie."

Jose thanked her but would not accept the gift. "You children love your pet," he said. "I find another soon. Now you ready to go before sun get hot? Not far. You rest while I get horses up."

To raise Mousie and Magpie was no easy matter, and Dick winced as Jose tugged the reins and beat them with the unstrung bow he had picked up. What water remained was not sufficient for two beasts almost dead from thirst, but Jose shared it to the last drop, and first Mousie then Magpie staggered to their feet.

The children felt very weak but managed to mount their horses and at a walking pace followed Jose's mustang until camp was reached, where they were soon the centre of a gaping crowd of women and children.

"Ha-ha!" smiled the Spaniard, as his wife kissed all three in turn, rather to Dick's disgust. "You plenty company now, Carlota—four bambino and a dog. No more thieving now."

"Has he been naughty already?" asked Tony, now well again, as he patted Wolf.

"No, no, little boy," laughed the man. "I mean two-legged thief. Ho-ho! Eli!" he waved to the old scout who had just ridden up and was staring at the rescued ones. "See what I find?"

The trapper slid from his horse and came forward scowling. He had found old tracks of unshod ponies away to the south, and the sight of Indian children aroused his suspicions, but after hearing Dick's story Eli looked relieved.

"Arrowhead, eh?" he said, pulling off his wide-brimmed hat and touching his bald crown. "You see anything of a lovely silky scalp in his teepee?"

F   81

"I saw many," Dick answered with a smile, amused at the old man's expression, "one scalp was long haired and white as snow—would that be yours?"

The group howled with delight at Dick's retort, and Eli chuckled.

"The Pawnees evidently did not take your wits away, boy. So you lived with Otter's squaw. I remember her—peevish old witch she was——"

"Gran treated us kindly," said May, not liking these rough people, "and adopted us. We came away because Redfeather——"

"*That* conceited hare-brained imp!" cried Eli. "Ha-ha! I knew him—he was a little boy when I was a prisoner, and the cruellest of the gang—always prodding me with a knife point and putting hot cinders under my feet as I lay bound. But tell me—do the Pawnees ever ride into the desert?"

"Sometimes," answered Dick. "If you've found Indian tracks—maybe they were searching for us."

"It is possible," Eli stroked his chin thoughtfully. "You have crossed only a corner of this desert, although you didn't know it, lucky for you. But make yourselves at home. . . ."

"Are we far from Nebraska?" asked May. "We are on our way to Riverside Ranch—our father is Judge Warner."

Many of the onlookers grinned, and as by now the other scouts had ridden up, some of the men exchanged curious glances. Three of them were

'Wanted'—their names were on posters at sheriffs' doors.

"We've heard of him," said the tall lancer, sucking a tooth. He also was 'Wanted' for desertion.

"Thousands of miles from Nebraska, my dears," exaggerated Eli; but sharp May saw several onlookers wink at each other, and felt relieved.

"Anyway," she said, "we thank you for finding us. Which way are you travelling?"

"To the gold fields," said Eli, his eyes lighting up as he pointed westwards. "We are the advance party of the Golden Army. The main body, a convoy of hundreds of prairie schooners, is coming on behind. We are waiting for them before striking into the desert. Why, bless you, half America is on the move. It wouldn't surprise me if Judge Warner came rolling up with the main party."

Several of the listeners thought this a good joke and tittered, but May and Dick did not. Tony was a little apart, showing young Toldo his specimens. "However," Eli concluded, filling a corn-cob pipe, "we'll see you get safely across the desert this time."

"Thank you," said Dick, rather coolly, "but we prefer to go the other way——"

"Not to be thought of," said Eli, grinning at the 'Wanted' men. "Your Pa would lynch us if we allowed you to leave the safety of the wagon train. So that's settled. You come and live with me," he said to Dick, "the little lad stays with Toldo; as for the girl—there's an old gipsy woman who is ill in that corner wagon and needs help. Off you go."

When the people had returned to their wagons, May and Dick whispered together.

"I don't quite like these folk," said May. "I overheard two women say something about . . . reward. They intend to hold us in the hope of getting money."

"I'd the same suspicion," said Dick. "We're to become bait to force dollars from Dad. However, we are safe until the Golden Army arrives—then we'll try to slip away."

When May Warner saw the gipsy woman lying amidst a pile of dirty pots and pans and oddments her soul filled with disgust. Madame Fortunia was not so old either. Like the rest in the camp her imagination had been fired by thoughts of easy gain at the gold fields and she had set off with her actor husband who had since died. Madame Fortunia, too, had been on the stage and had with her a few fancy dresses and wigs in a large wicker basket, the idea being that they could earn a living by giving performances en route.

Although far from being pleased with their new surroundings, the three children went cheerfully about their business. Dick took charge of their two mounts along with Eli's mustang, and with rest, water and good pasturage Mousie and Magpie soon recovered their good spirits.

Mousie was now accustomed to the feel of the bit

84

in his mouth, but when on the second day Dick was
ordered by Eli to go to the farrier's wagon to get the
colt fitted with shoes, Mousie did not submit without
a little unpleasantness, although the carving away of
some of the hoof and the hammering in of nails did
not pain him. How heavy and clumsy he felt with
pieces of iron to walk on, but he soon found out that
sharp flints no longer hurt and in time became used
to the strange things on his feet. Magpie was already
shod, so only needed her worn shoes replaced. As
Dick led the horses away, he chuckled to Mousie,
"Trapper Eli is thinking you'll travel across the
stony Desert of Death easier in horse-shoes, but I've
other ideas, chummy."

In such a cramped space the Warners often met

together when work was finished. Indeed there was little to do for anyone and the waiting period became irksome. Tony was kindly treated and well fed and romped with the Spanish boy and Wolfie. Dick took sentry duty in his turn and kept a better lookout than some of the men who, rendered careless by inaction, dozed at their posts.

Knowing Indian ways Dick was not content to sit on the wagon looking across the desert, as the soldier and some of the others did. The chaparral was thick with cactus, sage bushes and boulders, excellent cover for prowling Redmen. On moonless nights it would be an easy matter for an enemy to creep almost up to the wagon wheels.

CHAPTER XIII

"THE INDIANS ARE HERE!"

ONE night Dick went scouting Indian fashion, prowling around the camp and out into the chaparral. To pass the time in camp he had made for himself an Indian head-dress which he wore when away from camp. He knew, too, that if Indians did come around, the war-bonnet would be a useful disguise in the darkness.

On this particular night Dick's suspicions were aroused at once by the absence of lurking coyotes. He crept around on all fours, being too cunning to allow his head to be outlined against the sky. There was no moon, but the sky was starlit; the time, he judged, within two hours of sunrise—just the time Redskins creep up to spring a surprise attack, when the White men are in deepest sleep.

His watch over, Dick worked back towards camp, already within sight. He could see the rounded canvas covers blotting out a section of sky. Suddenly his pulses began to beat quicker as he fixed his eyes on a particular sage bush—a most active bush because it moved, very slowly to be sure, but enough for an 'Indian' boy's sharp eyes; and as he crouched there, other bushes moved up a pace: the whole chaparral was bewitched—and sheltering under each bush was a Redskin.

Dick knew that trick and was rising to go when a hand reached out and gripped his arm.

"Wagh!" a warrior whispered a warning into his ear. "Keep down . . . it is not time . . . yet."

"I know," Dick answered in the Indian language, "I am only moving nearer."

The night was too dark to make out anything but a black shape topped with feathers, but Dick felt sure he recognised the Brave by his voice: he was one of Redfeather's friends, by name Antelope because he was fleet of foot.

So these were Arrowhead's warriors, thought Dick. What a strange mischance. Angry at the escape of the Palefaces and suspicious of Gran Otter, Chief Arrowhead had decided to go at once on their trail, but in the forest the tracks of three children, a horse and dog had vanished. The result was that the Young Braves came upon the Warners' tracks by accident in the desert.

"Who is my brother?" asked the suspicious warrior.

Dick was in a fix, not knowing who had been sent out. He knew the names of all in the Pawnee camp and choosing at random answered, "Beaver"—a young Indian not very popular with Redfeather's set.

Warner felt his arm released. "Hough!" came the ejaculation. "Has not Beaver wandered too far? His party should be back in the forest."

Dick was saved by a Whuff! from the caravan, as Wolf, sniffing the well-remembered Indian scent, gave a yap of pleasure.

"Hist, Antelope!" whispered Dick, and at mention of his name the Brave appeared satisfied and faded away into the darkness, and Dick did too, at the stoop, straight for the camp, tearing off his war-bonnet as he ran to prevent being mistaken for an enemy.

Over the chained wheels he sprang into the wagon where the soldier was on sentry duty, and there he was—asleep with rifle on knee.

"Wake up! Indians!" Dick gave the deserter a push which sent him sprawling, and passed across to Eli's wagon.

"Wake! Wake!" he called out. "Eli—the Indians are here!"

There is dread magic in the word 'Indians,' and the old scout was awake instantly and outside the van almost before Dick had jumped into the next and shaken the occupants into action.

All this was not done without noise; sleeping dogs, trodden on by Dick, whuffed and snarled; a pet parrot belonging to Madame Fortunia awoke and ordered Dick to "Make less noise there! Go out! Tell your fortune, pretty one?" and Wolfie was prancing with excitement at the end of his chain.

These sounds were sufficient to warn the prowling Redskins that they were discovered, and one, Antelope, wished he'd kept a firm hold of the strange 'Indian.'

Suddenly from the chaparral came the shrill cry of the war-eagle, as Redfeather, the leader, by no means in the front rank, gave the prearranged call, and as

89

one man, threescore Braves bounded to their feet and rushed the caravans, yelling their blood-chilling war-whoop as they ran:

WHOOH-OOH! WHOOH-AH! YEEP! YEEP!

If an attack came, Dick had been told to stand by his sister and stay in the gipsy's van. Being accustomed to Indian ways, the shrill war-whoop had little effect on their nerves, but Madame Fortunia had turned pale, and for some reason only known to herself, had clutched the parrot as a kind of lucky mascot, and Polly, none too pleased, was filling the air with her own war-cry: "Scree—ch! Pretty Poll —Squawk! Be quiet! Tell your fortune, lady . . .?"

At any other time Dick and May would have been

amused, but along with the other children of their own ages, they had been allotted the duty of fire fighters and so left the wagon. In an Indian attack, the danger from burning arrows is always present.

With brimming canvas buckets ready, the children waited beside the spring, while the very young, including Tony and the Spanish child, lay face downwards on their wagon floors, some of them adding frightened yells to the din of battle. Tony was not alarmed, having often heard savage war-dances, and did his best to soothe his little companion. "There's nothing to be scared of. Who cares for a few Indians? Not me!"—remarks which made Jose, blazing away at every feathered head, laugh grimly.

To face a ring of rifle fire is not the Redskin way of fighting and after the first rush had been checked, they fell back into the chaparral, and from behind rocks and bushes kept up a fire of arrows and spears. They had learnt the Paleface way of making fire with flint, steel and tinder, and of a sudden the dry chaparral burst into flame at many points, followed by a dense cloud of smoke as the bushes caught alight. This was the dangerous moment. Fiery arrows began to flit through the smoke and two canvas covers were set on fire, and it was the children's turn to be busy, scampering to and fro with splashing buckets and handing them up to the women to extinguish the flames. Already the vans were prickly as porcupines with feathered arrows, and there were casualties. Old Eli roared like a bison as a war-arrow plugged his left arm, but he pulled it out quickly, hoping the fire-hardened point was not poisoned. Three other men were hit and one woman as she reached up with a bucket, but only the soldier's wound was serious—a spear thrust in the back—and he was carried to the 'casualty' wagon where women rendered first aid.

In the smoke and confusion of battle, the soldier's wagon was left unguarded and the attackers were quick to seize their chance: a dozen painted warriors mounted the chained wheels and were through, thus taking the defenders in the rear.

A desperate hand-to-hand conflict now took place in the fog of smoke so dense that only by the war-bonnets of the Redskins could Eli and those still in the combat distinguish friend from foe. The scared women and small children had been ordered to retreat to the boulders behind the gipsy's wagon, and all had gone there except Tony and the Spanish child. When Jose had become a tomahawk casualty, his wife had left her own van to go to his aid, so that for a few minutes the safety of the bambino was in the hands of seven-year-old Tony Warner.

For one so young he kept very calm and played the Indian game of lying 'dead coon.' With a rug over them they lay still as wax, and when a warrior stepped on Tony's back he did not cry out. Thus it was that when Dick, clearing the vans, looked into Jose's, he thought it was vacant and passed on.

A sensation of growing heat round Tony's bare toes

made him risk a peep under a corner of the rug and he found that the van floor was on fire.

"Rouse up, kiddie," he said, "unless you want roast toes for breakfast. We'll have to find another wigwam."

Throwing off the rug, he grasped the child and sprang up, but the smouldering floor was now charred and weak, and at the first step, down they went between the iron-shod wheels. Shaken, but unhurt, Tony pulled the boy to his feet and with bent heads they passed from wagon to wagon through the tunnel of wheels until, noticing a van drawn up beside the rocks a short distance away, the two raced across and climbed in. It was the gipsy's van, seemingly empty, until a movement of a curtain across one end showed where the terrified Madame was hiding.

Quick as thought Tony opened the lid of a large wicker basket and lifting the youngster inside, jumped in himself and lowered the lid. Burrowing like bunnies, the little lads wriggled their bodies among the contents and lay quiet—and only just in time.

CHAPTER XIV

LOVELY 'SCALPS'

THROUGH a gap in the wicker-work Tony saw a painted warrior peering into the wagon. It was Eagle Eye, and a horrible sight he looked daubed with red and white lines of warpaint, but Tony was used to this and kept calm. Knife in hand Eagle Eye vaulted inside and grinned as he caught sight of so many pretty things which Madame used to tell fortunes: globes of glass, strings of bright beads and other aids with which she deceived the ignorant gold seekers.

Eagle Eye was admiring a glass globe as large as a melon when a shrill voice made him give a start of surprise. "Put that down!" ordered the voice. "Go and wash—dirty face. Tell your fortune, pretty boy——"

SMASH! went the crystal globe, as Eagle Eye let it go, amazed at the sight of a talking green bird on a perch.

Polly screeched and rattled on: "Careless fel-low. Go and wash. Give Polly a kiss."

For a moment the warrior turned as though to run from such "heap strange magic," but catching sight of the wicker basket, his eyes lighted up with greed as he stepped across and threw back the lid.

What a sight for a bold warrior! Lovely 'scalps.'

He reached down and hauled out one of Madame Fortunia's wigs and stroked the silky curls. Not even Arrowhead had such magnificent scalps in his wigwam. Quickly untying his feathered war-bonnet he took it off and fitted the wig and admired himself in Madame's mirror hanging on a nail.

It was a desperate moment for the two children buried deep in the pile of 'props'—as theatrical goods are called—but Tony had to suppress a giggle at the comical sight Eagle Eye presented with the long curls dangling down his painted cheeks.

"Ugh! Heap good!" ejaculated the delighted warrior, returning to the basket and helping himself to a long-haired cavalier wig tied with ribbon. Exchanging wigs he thrust the first into his belt and lifted up a third. This was different—a Chinaman's pigtail with yellow mask to fit over the head. Eagle Eye had seen many scalps, but none with face attached and with a yelp of dismay dropped it and sprang back. He could not pale under his war-paint, but his knees shook with alarm. Magic indeed! A scalp with face left on and a magic bird jumping about on its perch and talking Paleface words —what a bird to amuse the Pawnee papooses.

Eagle Eye crossed the van and noticing the curtain drew it back and disclosed the crouching form of Madame.

He yapped like a dog sighting a juicy bone, and rushing in seized the terrified gipsy by the hair in

order to get a real scalp, but before his knife could be used—*her hair came off of its own accord*, and Polly, enraged at seeing her mistress in danger, sprang on Eagle Eye's neck and clawed him savagely.

With a yell the startled Brave dropped the wig and was out of the van in the shake of a rabbit's tail, forgetting in his haste that he still wore the cavalier's wig.

An hour had passed and the camp was quiet. The fight was finished and the Redmen victorious. Down by the spring lay Eli and several other men, bound with rawhide ropes; the women and children were herded among the rocks, guarded by armed warriors. All the horses, cattle and wagon mules were being driven off to the Indian camp; every van not burnt out was being plundered—except one, Madame's, but she was not there. Eagle Eye had summoned up enough courage to fetch her and she was a prisoner too. But no other warrior dare enter her van although all had looked in and marvelled at the strange things and still stranger bird; these now belonged to Eagle Eye and not even Redfeather dare break Indian rules. Now that danger was over he was well to the fore, stalking around in his feathered bonnet (his father had made him a Brave) and insulting the women. When he saw May Warner his eyes lit up with savage hate as he gloated in the Pawnee language, "Ha! We meet again, Blossom. So the Paleface girl did not like the Pawnee camp, eh?"

"I hated it," answered May with spirit.

"Ha-ha! But she will see it again before the moon is very old. Is not Blossom pleased to see Redfeather such a fine warrior?" he boasted, throwing out his chest and fingering his war-bonnet.

"I guess you got that head-dress dishonestly," said May meaningly. "Doesn't it prick you—like thorns?"

Redfeather knew what she meant and hurried away.

And still in the basket crouched two small forms, half smothered but uncaptured and unafraid because Tony made fun of everything.

During a quiet period they crept out and spying through a slit in the canvas cover, could see the prisoners lying bound, the Pawnee campfires out in the chaparral as they cooked food, several warriors sitting around smoking pipes; others attended to wounded comrades. The smoke of battle had cleared away revealing pale blue sky.

There was food and water in the gipsy's wagon, so the two boys made themselves comfortable, although Tony kept a sharp lookout and when a Redskin came anywhere near their wagon—back into the basket they hopped.

So the day passed and night came on. Polly, also fed, was asleep on her perch. The camp was quiet. Out on the plain the Pawnees, gorged with food and dazed with the gold seekers' strong drink, lay around their burnt-out fires, all except a few sentries half asleep and fuddled.

Eli and Jose—both roughly bandaged—and others unwounded (three men were dead, including the soldier) still lay bound and stiff as boards and tortured by thirst, having lain in the hot sun all day. Eli was in an angry mood, blaming the Warners for the defeat of the wagon train by bringing the Pawnees into the desert. It was true that the elder boy had warned the camp, though rather strange that he was not among the prisoners, nor was his young brother Antony. Queer . . .

Eli's thoughts were interrupted by a sound close to his head, no louder than a cat makes stalking a sparrow. "A rattlesnake," he groaned inwardly, but warm breath on his ear calmed the trapper's fears.

"Sh-h!" came a soft voice. "Don't move . . . I'm cutting your ropes."

Owing to cramp, Eli was hardly aware that he possessed limbs, but soon a tingling in his wrists showed that he was free. He watched the dark shadow flit from one prisoner to the next and sink to the earth when an Indian moved. As feeling returned, Eli felt something else and his fingers closed round the butt of a revolver which Tony had picked up and loaded.

To and fro went Tony Warner, silent as a foraging mouse, cutting ropes and pushing knives, revolvers and tomahawks, left by the Redskins, within reach of prisoners' fingers. He was not the only prowler either. Unknown to each other Dick and Tony were on the same game. When Dick had seen that the battle was lost, and knowing he could do no good by being captured, he had climbed the rocks and hidden in a cranny, and at dusk had searched the camp for fire-arms and had six rifles loaded and ready stacked under one of the wagons. On his rounds Dick caught sight of a form slinking near the gipsy's van, and so did Tony as he was about to climb in. Both went to earth like hares between the wheels. Being in a patch of shade they could see nothing clearly, but each knew the other was there. Tony bunched himself up hoping to be mistaken for a skulking dog, and to give this impression growled softly as he and his brother had often done when playing in the woods.

Dick chuckled, recognising the sound and, feeling

mightily glad that Tony was still alive, answered with a low Meow-w!

The two crawled up to each other and sat laughing silently, as Indians do, as they felt each other's arms and hands and in whispers explained what they had done.

"Good for you, little one," breathed Dick into Tony's ear. "You deserve a whole war-bonnet of honour feathers for that."

"I've got one," said Tony, thinking of Eagle Eye's head-dress still in Madame's caravan.

"Honest?" asked Dick.

"You'll see. Creep up here, but be quiet . . . we mustn't wake the heap magic bird."

Dick soon understood and patted Tony for a brave fellow as he tried on Eagle Eye's bonnet and nearly disappeared amidst a cascade of feathers.

"What name are you taking, o' brother Brave?" asked Dick, admiring Tony standing in a patch of starlight shining through the torn canvas.

"Pretty boy!" said a voice from the darkness, which startled both of them, so interested had they been in the war-bonnet. Dick rushed forward to throw the cover over Polly and stop her chatter, but too late. She gave a shriek like a steam whistle, and as though it were a signal, from the encampment came a rush of feet and a volley of revolver shots.

The Redskins, drowsy with food and drink, had no chance and went down like skittles under the rapid fire from the enraged miners' six-shooters.

Those out in the chaparral jumped on to their mustangs and circled the camp, but by this time Dick's store of rifles had been distributed and many riderless horses showed evidence of accurate shooting by the Whites.

At daybreak the gold seekers had a busy time clearing up the camp and repairing several wagons not too badly burned. Those belonging to the soldier and his dead comrades were given to the survivors who had lost theirs. Such rough folk spent no time in regrets and buried the dead without ceremony, and for two days the usual camp routine went on. Not a word was said about the bravery of the 'Pawnee papooses,' but men boasted about what they had done; women, too, especially the gipsy, hoping for business.

"Was I afraid of that painted fool?" she shrilled, shaking a doubled fist. "Not I. I smacked his war-painted face, I did."

"You gave him a *wigging*, eh?" called out Eli, who had seen Eagle Eye in his new war-bonnet of curls—a remark which made the men guffaw, but was hint enough to Madame Fortunia that it would be wise to calm down.

Carlota was grateful to Tony for saving her child and so was the bandaged Jose. "You come with us," he said. "We'll keep you safe. Scouts say the Main Body be here to-night—then we go across the desert to get rich."

Dick happened to be there and May too, helping to tidy the new wagon.

"See here, Senor Toldo," said Dick earnestly. "You've just said how thankful you were that little Tony . . . er . . . well . . . I don't like to boast, but he saved the camp—didn't he?"

"Si, si (yes), he grand lad. Did I not tell those greedy camp boys to give up that war-bonnet he wanted?"

"You did, Senor, but we don't want to go gold seeking. We want to go home to Riverside Ranch. Will you help us to get away some dark night?"

"No, no, it too risky. The Sioux catch you again. After we get rich . . . we all go east. We take you to your father——"

Dick knew what Jose wanted—a reward—and said no more, and when at sunset hundreds of prairie schooners came crowding up, their chance of escape seemed more remote.

It was a scene never to be forgotten. In all directions the chaparral was dotted with white canvas tops, the wagon wheels buried in sage bushes. There was no danger now, and fires were lighted and meals cooked. What a medley of folk of all nationalities—a town seemed to have sprung to life. Several wagons were really travelling shops and sold goods at high prices. At each halt a large oblong tent was erected and became a saloon to serve drinks, which made men quarrelsome, and shots were fired, sometimes fatally. At night flares were lit within, and the gambling tables filled with miners, cow-punchers, lumberers, tinkers, tailors, soldiers, sailors—as yet no rich men but many poor—all fired with the one idea—to get rich—because gold had been discovered in the mountains out West. Not all were rough men. Some had come for adventure, others to send news to newspapers, but taking all in all the camp was no place for three lost children.

About a week later while Old Eli was playing poker in the saloon, Dick slipped across to Jose's van where he'd seen May enter a few minutes previously. She was putting the Spanish child to bed. Jose and Carlota were 'in town' at the side-shows where Madame Fortunia was giving a third-rate theatrical performance with some new-found friends.

"Pretty Poll, pretty Poll!" said Dick with a grin, poking his head through the canvas.

"Oh, be quiet," said May. "I'm tired of such doings. You'd be amazed how silly folk are, listening open mouthed to Madame's nonsense—and giving money to her."

"She'll get richer that way than by gold digging," chuckled Dick. "Hullo, Wolfie!" patting the dog. "Still all alive-o! I guess you've fought all the dogs in town, eh? Where is your master Tony, the bold Indian warrior?"

"Here!" called out the brother, entering at that moment. "You've missed all the fun, Dickie—I've been to see the prisoners."

"Which prisoners?"

"Three Redskins caught by a scouting party—one is Redfeather."

Dick whistled. "Redfeather?—well, of all the—what will they do with him?"

"They've done it," said Tony turning away.

Dick did not ask for details, but later found out that a party of Mexican cow-punchers had surprised the retreating war-party out in the chaparral and during a running fight Redfeather's mustang had been shot and himself captured with two others. They had been brought into 'town' and Judge Lynch had done the rest. The three captives had been hanged from one of the wagons—and only Redfeather had pleaded for his life.

"Somehow," said Dick to May, after telling her the news, "I can't help feeling sorry, although he was a dreadful cheat and boaster."

May sighed. "It's a pity Red and White can't live at peace. There is plenty of land for all. Why don't the Whites mark off a section as a sort of Indian Park and let them live on it?"—a wish which came true not long afterwards when the Oklahoma Reservation was set aside for Pawnees for all time.

In secret the Warners plotted to escape while they had time.

"They've no right to make us go gold seeking if we don't want," said Dick. "When I mention going eastwards to Nebraska every one says, 'Too dangerous.' They say that Black Cloud's warriors are on the warpath trying to stop the railroad being built. Also there is Tiger Murrell's bandit gang in the mountains we have to cross."

"We'll risk it," said May, "rather than face that awful desert again."

"That's what I think," said Dick. "We must try to slip away to-night."

"Have we far to go?" asked Tony.

"I've been talking to the cowboys," Dick answered, "and we have only the State of Colorado to cross—not far if you say it quickly."

"Gracious!" exclaimed May. "Any deserts?"

"No, but we've some high mountains to climb and, as the Darkies sing, we've one more river to cross—many times."

"Can we take Mousie and Magpie?" asked Tony. "I can't walk all that way."

"You won't have to, brave warrior," smiled his

brother. "Sh-h! Canvas walls have ears and the child may not be asleep. I've got Mousie and Magpie ready, well fed, watered and rested, and to-night there's a late breaking-up party in the big saloon—everybody will be there—except three I know. So be ready in about an hour's time—dressed in your new clothes."

CHAPTER XV

HOMEWARD BOUND

"Funny," laughed Dick Warner, "three White people having to disguise ourselves as English."

He looked across at Magpie with May on the saddle. In her canary coloured shirt with green tie, riding breeches, spurred boots and spreading Stetson hat she was hardly recognisable as the Pawnee captive. Dick, too, looked a real cowboy in scarlet shirt, leather chaps and high-heeled Mexican boots with spur rowels as large as silver crowns on which tiny bells tinkled; a huge hat with snake-skin band shaded his tanned face. Tony, too, in trousers and shirt, was a little papoose no longer, although he had grumbled a little at the weight of the boots. All three had gathered up their new 'rig outs' with great caution. May, as Madame's assistant, had been given tips by clients, and spent the money at the shops. Dick had earned a few dollars by grooming horses, and a newspaper correspondent had given Tony a handful of coins for telling about how they had lived in captivity.

They had found no difficulty in leaving camp. Most folk were enjoying themselves for the last time before striking the desert trail. Eli had told Dick to see to the horses and he had obeyed, though not quite in the way the trapper meant.

During the hours of darkness they had made good progress and by dawn were miles away on the prairie and happy as larks. Indeed they sang like birds as they put their mounts into the long-distance lope, with Wolf trotting ahead.

"Now all together!" shouted Dick, beating time with his bow which he did not want to throw away:

> "*Come companions, join your voices,*
>   *Hearts with pleasure bounding;*
> *Sing we of this long ride,*
>   *When we get to Riverside,*
> *Joys of home sweet home resounding.*

> CHORUS: *Home! sweet home, with ev'ry pleasure,*
>   *Home! with ev'ry blessing crowned.*

Home! our best delight and treasure,
Home! the welcome strain resound.

Quit your weary Pawnee labours,
  Quit the camp fires burning;
Banish all cares aside,
  Welcome to Riverside,
Hearts for home and freedom yearning.

CHORUS: *Home! sweet home, with ev'ry pleasure,*
Home! with ev'ry blessing crowned.
Home! our best delight and treasure,
Home! the welcome strain resound."

Hope and the thought of their ranch spurred them
on, and after a day's ride they saw a pale blue splash
on the horizon which represented the high mountains
they had to cross. The open prairie provided plenty
of game and at each stream they came to, the horses
were well watered and Dick's canteen filled to the
brim. These occasions always brought a fresh out-
burst of song:

  " The Pawnees went in three by three,
    One more river to cross;
  Mousie and Magpie, Wolf as well,
    One more river to cross . . ."

So on they went with song and jest—a merry trio.
To reserve their provisions Dick shot a small deer
and they feasted on roast venison, and so did Wolf
until he could hardly waddle. At times they hid in
the grass to let suspected riders pass and only once

came near to discovery when a band of rough-looking men swished through the grass within a hundred yards of where they crouched.

"More of them suffering from gold fever," said May. "I wouldn't tackle that desert again for a fortune."

"Nor I," said Dick, "and they've a longer trail than we had. Hi-o! Off we go. *One more river to cross*. Come up, Mousie. Up, Magpie! Tony—where are you?"

"Here," cried the lad, appearing through the tall grass holding a toad as big as a pint mug. "Isn't this a beauty?"

"Ugh! Put it down," cried May, "you're always after live things. You'd have a prairie schooner full if we didn't watch you. What's that thing in your belt? A jack-rabbit-skin!"

She pulled it out and showed it to Dick who grinned and wrinkled his nose. "Not half cured," he plagued. "It will soon be full of maggots. Where did you get it?"

"One Jose caught for dinner and I cured the skin. I'm going to make Mam a purse from it. Don't throw it away!"

"You and your skins," said Dick, tossing it down.

"But for you I'd have had a grizzly bear-skin," cried Tony, taking up the rabbit pelt. "I wish we hadn't left . . ."

"All right," May interrupted, "we're tired of hearing about that bear-skin we left at the shack.

Come on! Up you get on to Magpie and kindly leave room for me."

They rode hard all day, but the mountains seemed as far off as ever. May mentioned this.

"The air is so clear," Dick explained, "besides—we are not making straight for the range."

"So I've noticed," May smiled. "Why?"

"Because one of those newspaper men told me that a railway crosses farther north—and I thought we'd buy tickets," he concluded with a grin.

These were the days when the Union Pacific Railroad was pushing westwards with as much speed as the Red men would allow, and during the children's year of captivity a line had been laid across the prairie to the mountains. The Indians gazed with awe at the iron horse snorting its way across their hunting grounds and did all they could to obstruct the White men's work. The telegraph beside the line was pulled to pieces as soon as erected: poles were knocked down and wires broken; squaws were fond of the green glass insulators fitted to the poles; rails were prised up and trees placed on the track to wreck the trains. Engine driver, fireman and guard had to be ready to pump lead into galloping Sioux. At scattered intervals were Halts with a water-tank, stack of fuel and sometimes a rough shack labelled Telegraph Office and a Y-switch on to a siding for loading cattle. Between Halts stretched the rolling prairie or alkali flats.

Of course Dick had no hope of riding on the

railway, but he knew that the rails crossed the mountains at the easiest place and meant to find it; otherwise they might search for months for a place to cross. There were peaks ten thousand feet above sea level, deep canons, and impassable rushing streams. To get lost in some lonely gorge meant starvation; to linger on the plain was just as dangerous. The children were crossing the hunting ground of the Sioux—a tribe more warlike than Pawnees. A certain type of the White men they met would have robbed the children of much-prized rifle, revolvers and horses, and always were the dreaded bandit bands, enemies of all.

That was why the Warners trusted no one, relying on themselves, keeping a sharp eye on the horizon and squatting in the grass at the first sign of human life, a precaution which lost them valuable time, so that it became customary to travel at night with the large September moon lighting up the plain.

But weather was not always favourable. As they neared the heights rain-storms became frequent, sometimes with thunder and lightning. They thought little of this but disliked getting their clothes wet. Dick was good at forecasting a change in the weather, so that shelter could be found or made by stretching blankets across the kneeling bodies of the horses and crouching underneath. By day the sun soon dried the blankets.

One hot night Dick had scented an oncoming storm and called a halt.

"Sister," he said, "have you noticed anything?"

"Yes—a tree at last."

"Not so. Thou art losing thy Pawnee eyesight. Ever see a tree so straight of trunk? Yon's a telegraph pole."

"And a telegraph means civilisation," said May excitedly. "We'll be able to send a message home. Hurrah! Hurrah!"

"Silence, squaw," said Dick, who sometimes spoke 'Indian' for fun. "One cannot tap a wire and send a message—one needs a telegraph office. Thou art like the nigger who hung his old boots on the wire to send them to be repaired quicker. Now silence while Great Chief Dickie goes to scout."

Although he was in joking mood, his heart was lighter at sight of that pole. It told him that he'd located the railway and the pass across the high mountains. He was, in fact, more fortunate than he expected, for within the space of a few minutes, they crept cautiously up to a tiny railroad Halt and dismounted.

May, Tony, Mousie and Magpie, not forgetting Wolf, sank down among the bushes while Dick went forward to scout. He was soon back.

"Not a soul on the premises," he said, "everything locked up, not a glimmer of light, but—I've found shelter."

"Oh, good!" cried May. "Where?"

"Beggars can't be choosers," he replied, "but even a cattle truck——"

H 113

It took them all their time not to cheer. A cattle truck! Why, it was luxury! The deserted station composed of a few log huts seemed to breathe a whisper of that magic word—Home.

Leading the horses, they skirted the Halt, passed a huge water-tank, and on a siding found several empty trucks with sloping runways for the cattle to enter. Luckily Magpie had travelled in railway trucks, so gave no trouble, and Mousie followed with little more than a snort of nervousness. To prevent their straying, Dick let the wooden runway drop and almost closed the sliding door. It was a large truck, partitioned for several animals, so that Mousie and Magpie were placed at the far end, the saddles and baggage in the middle section, leaving the other end for their own occupation.

"This is splendid," cried May, feeling around and arranging the straw and sacks for beds, "and only just in time. Listen to the patter of rain on the roof. We'd have got a real soaking. Now for supper and a real comfortable sleep."

CHAPTER XVI

TROUBLE FOR MAY

MAY WARNER was the first to hear the throb-throb of the approaching locomotive and woke with a start.

"Dick!" she nudged her brother. "Listen!"

He sat up rubbing his eyes; then all jumped to their feet and, keeping out of the rain, peeped round the door of their shelter. Already they could see the bright headlight which turned the wet rails into shining bands of white; chuff-chuff—chuffa-chuff! panted the engine, then came to rest, its air-brake pumping deep breaths.

Across the slants of rain the children saw a man jump down, pass in front of the engine, and disappear into the darkness. On the footplate the fireman's face glowed red as he opened a furnace door to stoke up. The sight was so new and interesting to the children's 'Indian' eyes that they stood like statues, watching the guard unhook the engine which chuffed off and backed down the siding; came the clang-clang of buffers and a jerk which made the horses restive and Dick had to run to soothe them.

A man swinging a lantern came along the line and crossed to a siding and they heard the bang of doors as the other empties were closed.

"Luckily the train is going eastwards," said May, still peering out. "What shall we say to him?"

"Ask him the cost of tickets for three children, two horses and one pup to the nearest point to Riverside Ranch," Dick called out. "Tell him Dad will pay. You go—I dare not leave hold of Mousie."

"Right-o!" May jumped out and passed down the line of wagons, but nowhere could she see the man with the lantern who, having noticed that all doors were now closed, had hurried out of the rain back to the Halt.

The girl was accustomed to the forest and prairie but not to railway tracks and in the darkness tripped up over an obstruction and fell full length beside the line. At that moment the engine gave a chuff—CHUFF! and began to move.

"May!" called out Dick. "Come back! The train's moving—you'll be left——"

She heard nothing except the throb of iron wheels, the hiss of steam and the noise of the storm. For once she was horribly scared as the wagons slipped past her prone body, gathering speed each instant. . . .

Dick had to make a quick decision. Leaving the horses he sprang to the door with the intention of helping May, but if he had jumped out Tony would have been left . . . and the train was gathering speed . . . he was too late. . . .

The two boys stood looking at each other, stunned into silence, listening to the bobbety-clang! bobbety-clang! chuff! of the freight train. There was no way

116

of stopping it—a string of wagons was between them and the driver.

"Whatever will she do?" Tony found his tongue at last, but Dick was too miserable to reply and only shook his head. He was thinking of May, with no money or food, left at a deserted Halt and another train might not pass for days, and there were bands of Sioux always on the prowl. . . .

Acting on a sudden idea Dick sprang to the door. "I'm going to climb along the wagons and stop the train. Mind you don't fall out."

It was a desperate attempt from the start and Dick knew it, yet fear for his sister spurred him on. Rain lashed his body and wind tore at his clutching fingers to loosen them. Except for the red glare of the engine far in front he was groping in jet darkness, feeling for hand-holds and swaying dangerously over the dizzy gulf between his truck and the next.

What to do he knew not. The space above the buffers was too wide to lean across, yet he must attempt something. If he sprang and missed his hand-hold he would drop to the metals—maybe be pounded into pulp—in any case left behind—like poor May.

Reckless lad! He risked all and sprang—missed— and down he went——

A large iron hook saved his life and there he hung, swaying over the track, his legs flailing around for foot-hold; and to make matters more terrifying, at that moment the train thundered on to an iron

bridge, and looking down Dick could see nothing but girders between him and the gaping black gulf.

How he escaped death Dick never quite knew. Vaguely he remembered clawing around, hanging to wet slippery buffers, and swinging himself up on to his own truck. Wet to the skin and trembling he located the partly open door and the watchful Tony helped him in.

"No chance," Dick panted, shaking himself like a dog. "Black as a wolf's throat out there and I was nearly . . . blown off the train."

He took a spare cowboy shirt from a package and, after drying himself as best he could, put it on.

For once, despair entered their hearts. To be separated was worse than captivity, the desert or the mining camp; a sad end to all their efforts to escape: two of them going east at fifty miles an hour towards Nebraska and Riverside Ranch, and poor May . . . left . . . alone. . . .

About an hour later the moon broke through the rolling rain-clouds and the boys saw they were in the mountains, with high peaks on all sides and fir forests. The train rattled over iron trestle bridges where frothing yellow streams could be seen hundreds of feet below. Dick did his best to attract the attention of the driver by leaning out and waving a piece of sacking, but was unobserved. The cars swayed and clanged with such a rattle that Dick's idea of firing a few shots from his revolver was given up as hopeless.

"Well, Tony boy," he said, "it's no use being downhearted. The train has to stop some time, so there's nothing we can do except wait. Cheer up, kid. We've been in worse fixes than this."

"But . . . *May*!" choked out Tony, his eyes bright with unshed tears.

"I know," Dick soothed. "It was my foolish fault—I should have gone myself. Anyway, we'll soon be across these mountains and when we get to Nebraska we'll ask Dad to charter a special train to fetch our May Blossom. There's nothing we can do —so we might as well sit down—and wait."

CHAPTER XVII

"DEAD LADS TELL NO TALES"

"HULLO!" exclaimed Dick Warner, starting into wakefulness, "the train rocked us to sleep." Tony was sitting up picking straw from his clothes. Through the gap between the sliding door and jamb they could see the level plain again, now sunlit, and a patch of blue sky; but what seemed strange was that the train had stopped. Both jumped to their feet and looked out.

"Hurrah! A station and men and carts," cried Tony, pointing down the track. "Now we're all right."

"We're all wrong, sonny boy," Dick answered grimly, pulling him back.

"Why do you say that? Oh, look! Has there been an accident? There's a man lying close to the line. Is that why we stopped?"

"I guess that shot woke us up," Dick answered, having seen more than his brother. "Keep your head in—we're out of luck."

"Is it—a hold-up?" asked Tony excitedly.

"I'm afraid so, and they've shot the driver and captured the fireman and guard. They've taken them to the telegraph operator's hut."

By now armed men had begun to search the

wagons, and boxes and bales were being hauled to the doors ready to be collected by the four-wheeled carts. Each time the men opened an empty car their tempers became worse. It was easy to see what had happened: the bandits had captured the station and shot down the driver when he refused to be held up. The train was carrying nothing valuable so that the guard had been riding in the cab for company on the long stretches.

Dick knew it was useless to hide or run, but hid his guns under the straw and stood hands in pockets whistling *One more river to cross* as a rough-looking bandit sauntered up, pistol in hand.

"Good morning!" said Dick.

The man jumped and swung up his six-shooter to cover the van, but seeing only two boys, thrust his gun into the holster.

"And who are you?" asked the robber.

"Hoboes (tramps)," replied Dick with a shrug, "sneaking a ride. What station is this?"

"It's the station you come off," snarled the man, not liking Dick's cheery manner, "and the kid, too. Come out!—and keep that snarling cur quiet."

They caught Wolf and obeyed at once and stood on the track while the bandit searched among the straw and bundles and soon appeared, holding Dick's guns.

"Huh!" grunted the man. "Hoboes, eh?—with horses. Um! the grey's not so bad, but that old one's only fit for dog meat. Come on, now! No nonsense —what are you two kids doing here?"

"We've been prisoners among the Pawnees and——"

"No lies now," came the sneering interruption. "Better think up a more likely excuse for the boss."

"Who is the boss?" asked Dick, putting on a brave front, although badly scared.

The outlaw jumped down and thrust his unshaven jaw into Dick's face. "He's known as Tiger Murrell. Ever heard of him?"

Dick had: the leader of an outlaw gang wanted for cattle-rustling and horse stealing, and now, by the look of that prone body, for murder.

They watched the fellow examine another two trucks and then, after dragging a wooden crate labelled BACON to the door of the last freight car, climb down.

"Now, you kids," he ordered, "hop along to the shacks. Dead men—and lads—tell no tales. Smart now!"

The boys walked along the track and stood looking into the telegraph operator's hut. On the floor were the bound figures of the fireman, guard, and operator, and on a bench the outstretched form of the driver. A young bandit was plugging a wound in the man's shoulder, and, having his back to the boys, was unaware of their presence. Another robber was searching the hut for cash. Dick recognised him as Tiger Murrell from 'Wanted' posters he had seen before being taken prisoner by Pawnees. He looked a real ruffian, but said nothing to Dick and Tony, only flicking his thumb towards a waiting cart as indication of what they must do.

To load the carts did not take long, and the boys were bundled into one of them along with crates of tinned goods and bacon. Poor Wolfie had been kicked on to the alkali plain by a bandit, and the boys had lost sight of him. Mousie and Magpie, heavily loaded, had joined the string of mules.

The two boys remained silent as the cavalcade mounted into the hills. They were having dreadful luck, everything going wrong: poor May left alone on the other side of the mountains, and themselves prisoners; even if the ruffian's threat about dead boys telling no tales was bluff, they would surely be held for ransom—their father would have to pay thousands of dollars . . .

Dick's worries were interrupted by a ripple of excitement which ran along the cavalcade. Several bandits turned in their saddles and pointed down to the plain; then lashed the horses into greater efforts. Sioux, thought Dick, as he caught sight of a line of horsemen strung out like dots along the horizon. Even bandits were afraid of large war-parties, and he was relieved when the dots grew smaller and disappeared. To be captured again by savages would be almost as bad a fix as they were in—maybe worse.

It soon became obvious, however, that the gang was uneasy. Several times the leader called a halt and the men crowded together deep in argument but always on the alert. Far below were the matchbox-size station and the plundered freight train, and Dick wondered what would happen when the next express came thundering along.

Having come to a decision the men moved on, and to the boys' surprise left the main track and struck along a dangerous-looking path which led to an open cave with a high cliff above and a sheer precipice below. This was no robbers' hide-out, Dick knew, because anyone could find it, so that when the carts and mules were left loaded, he was not surprised. Judging by the way the outlaws examined rifles and revolvers they were expecting trouble, and all except one man mounted their horses and rode away.

He was a hard-faced, villainous-looking fellow, the type who could slit a throat and think nothing of it, and that was why he had been left behind. When he drew a bowie-knife and tested the edge with his thumb, the boys thought he was going to cut a plug of tobacco, but instead he approached the cart and ordered curtly: "Come down—and let's get the business done."

Although partly expecting the blow, the boys opened their eyes wide with horror. Surely he was not going to commit a double murder in that cold-blooded way, with no more feeling than killing chickens, and Dick stammered out: "W—wha—what business do you mean?"

"What do I mean?" repeated the grinning wretch as he flourished the knife. "I mean I'm going to cut your little windpipes and then you won't be able to tell any tales nor ask any more silly questions. Down you get! You are dead meat——"

"I don't think so," said a quiet voice from his rear. "Put up your hands—or *you* are dead meat!"

The man had swung round at the first word and his jaw dropped at sight of a cocked revolver ·45 held in a girl's steady hand.

"Hurrah, hurrah!" cried Dick. "Good old Blossom!"

He was off that cart quicker than a wink, and as the man dropped his knife to pull his guns, Dick sprang at him.

THUD! went his fist on a whiskery jaw and the man went down like a skittle in an alley. A flashing straight left it was, and Warner meant the blow to tell.

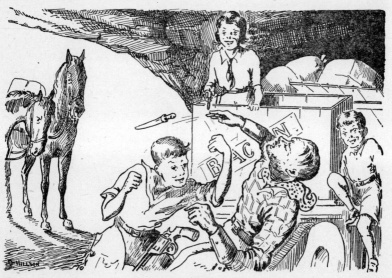

125

No Redfeather sparring, this—but a real knockout thump, and with three lives at stake he was quite justified. So dazed was the fellow that, as he fell, his two guns skiddered along the rocky floor.

May jumped down from her bacon crate and stood over him until Dick picked up the man's weapons. By this time Tony had climbed out of the cart and taken up the knife.

"Ha-ha!" gloated Dick Warner. "Lively bacon, wasn't it? If he moves, Tony boy, slit his little windpipe before he's time to ask any silly questions. Who's dead meat now, eh?"

"I was supposed to be," said May.

"Really, sister, this is a *gorgeous* surprise. This beats the old Medicine Man's conjuring tricks. How did you manage it?"

"I'll tell you *after* we've got the *business* done," she smiled sweetly at the seated bandit. "Hand one of those guns to Tony. He's small but I warn you, Mr. Throat Slitter, he has a temper like a grizzly bear, so if *you* don't want to become dead meat, sit quiet and enjoy the scenery. Dicky, there's a sack in my Aladdin's crate—fetch it, will you please?" with a wink. "Mr. Bandit might catch a chill sitting on the cold hard floor."

Dick obeyed and as he passed behind the man, popped the sack quickly over his head and grasped his windpipe through the cloth, while at the same time May called out, "If you wriggle—I'll shoot! Tony, stab him with that knife!"

Being blindfolded the man was unaware of three wide grins, and as he was a coward at heart submitted quietly while his arms and legs were tied with ropes from a pile in the cart and the sack made secure.

"Now that does look more like a side of bacon," said Dick. "What do you say, sister?"

"He'd look better inside his crate," she replied, "just as a precaution in case the other . . . er . . . hogs come back."

The crate was soon out of the cart, and with Tony's help, the outlaw was lifted inside and the lid nailed down. "That's how I travelled part of the way," said May, "so I know there's plenty of ventilation."

"However did you manage it?" asked Dick.

"I caught the last wagon as it rumbled past me, and having a bit of monkey in me climbed up, and as it didn't look too safe creeping along to you in the darkness, I went to sleep."

"If we'd only known," said Tony. "We've been worried to death."

"*Nearly* to death, my chick. Mr. Bacon there is our death expert—but I'll tell you later. If no one's around, we'll find another hotel. I never did like stone floors. Fetch the two M's along, Dicky, they're just outside and then we'll make our getaway."

CHAPTER XVIII

A DESPERATE RACE

"Look!" exclaimed May Warner as they click-clocked out of the cave. "We are only just in time."

In the distance on the plain below were several midge-size objects coming in their direction.

"Those Sioux returning," said Dick. "There'll be a bit of hard riding to do when we get on the level. Luckily Mousie and Magpie have had a good rest." He was on the colt with Tony up behind hanging to his revolver belt, leaving the old mare with only one weight to carry.

They were soon on the plain abreast the station and the derelict train, which reminded Dick of the imprisoned men.

"I'm going to do my good deed," he called out to May. "You ride on . . ."

May waved a hand to show she understood and put Magpie into a gallop, while Dick sprang down and dashed into the station, knife in hand.

"If you hurry," he said to the bound and gagged figures as he cut their ropes, "you've just time to run up to the cave. There are horses and guns, but mind you open that crate of bacon carefully—there's a live hog in it."

"Thanks, chum," said the telegraph operator.

"We'll manage now. If you are going to run for it—off you go. I've guns and shells hidden in the caboose over there—we'll fight them."

"We had no live pigs aboard," said the guard. "What do you mean, boy?"

"Whiskery Bill, the throat slitter," laughed Dick, halting at the door. "Look in the bacon crate—then you'll understand. Is Riverside Ranch this way?" he pointed ahead.

"Sure!" the operator answered, "keep right on...."

"Thanks," said Dick, mounting swiftly, and as Mousie's lively hoofs hit up a swirl of alkali dust, he heard the men call out:

"Good luck, sonny!"

May had been making good progress, but the colt soon overhauled her, and Dick reined in a little to keep abreast. Glancing backward he saw that the horsemen were much nearer and almost at the station. Not Indians either, but White men.

Immediately came the crack! crack! of rifle fire.

"Another five minutes, Tony boy," laughed Dick, "and we'd have been caught. Those bandits are back again. Stick on like a burr. This is the last lap —one good gallop and we'll be on our own land. Hi-o! for Riverside Ranch!"

Dick was being cheery for a purpose. They had a long, long way to go yet, but far in front was a range of hills with a peak like a tiny blue triangle which Dick had recognised as forming the ten-mile boundary of their ranch.

I

When he was sure of this, he shouted the news to May, and the three gave a cheer. Home at last, after wild adventures: Riverside Ranch and Mam and Dad, their ponies, cats and dogs. For twelve months the children had been Crusoes of the Prairie—now they were safe—or almost.

"Ride your hardest," encouraged Dick to his sister, aware that he was holding Mousie in. "The poor old mare is doing fine—but tickle her up a bit with the spur—the bandits are gaining on us."

He kept looking back every quarter mile and through the dust could see that the pursuers were pounding along at a fast pace. All were splendidly mounted and fine horsemen. If Magpie could only keep the pace.....

Already she was flagging and lathered in foam, a sure sign of distress. May rode her skilfully, easy on the rein, but ready to pull her out of each stumble; urging her on with gentle words and an encouraging pat now and again. Dick galloped up alongside and relieved May of the weight of her revolver belt, blanket and saddle bag; and for a time they thundered on, but Mousie was now overloaded with two humans to carry. It would be heart-breaking to fail at the last lap. The blue peak was now nearer and a line of cottonwood trees could be seen—the boundary of the Riverside Estate. Dick had often wondered what their home-coming would be like—but never imagined such a desperate race for life.

To ease the weight Dick dropped his rifle, groaning

inwardly; then May's heavy revolver and belt, only keeping his own; blankets followed and then he reached for Tony's special property, his bag of treasures: the simple toys made under Gran's direction, the pressed flowers and leaves and butterfly specimens, the pebbles and stones he used as marbles, the prized rabbit-skin for Mam's purse and a bedraggled folded war-bonnet looking like a chicken in the moult.

"Sorry, kid," said Dick, "all will have to go."

"Oh, Dickie!" cried Tony, "I'm sure that bit of weight won't matter."

"Weighs a ton," Dick bluffed. "Whatever have you got in it—a load of logs? Now, now, don't try to grab it—or you'll be off and then Mr. Bacon will try a little operation on your throat."

He tossed the bag into a thorny cactus.

Tony thumped his back—hard. "You are a bad, wicked brother," sobbed the little fellow in a temper, "and I don't like you. I was going to make a pur furse," he blundered in his distress.

Dick laughed. "You mean . . . *fur purse*." He was feeling the strain too and growing angry at Fate's trick: to be chased like foxes at the last few miles.

The pursuers were now very close, forming dim shapes in the dust cloud, a long line of them strung out, the foremost yelling like a Redskin and flourishing a lasso. The next behind was waving a revolver, and a shot rang out—then another——

Tony ducked and bumped his nose on Dick's

leather belt, and Dick hunched up his shoulders. It was not pleasant to be a target for yelling sharp-shooters, and he must keep an eye on poor Magpie—staggering now and panting for breath.

May knew that all would soon be over. Sweat was oozing from Magpie's saddle girth, and flecks of blood-streaked foam shot from her muzzle at every cough of the tired lungs . . . and then, like breaking a twig, the mare suddenly collapsed and slumped into the dust, her arched neck between quivering forelegs —a brave effort and gallant sacrifice to save her little human friends.

D·HILLSON

For a long time May had been expecting this to happen and rolled clear, shouting, "Ride on, Dick!" then ran to Magpie's tired head and clasped it in her arms.

"Thanks, old partner," she spoke into the twitching ears, "you've done your best. Goodbye," and May Warner, who seldom cried, dropped two big tears on Magpie's quivering white nose.

May glanced up as Dick came thundering back and dismounted, six-shooter in hand.

"Up you get, sis," he ordered, "and take Tony on —there's our fence only a hundred yards ahead. I'm going to stay and shoot it out."

"Go yourself," said May, standing fast.

"Now, don't be awkward," cried the elder boy. "Look! Here comes number one." He raised his gun and fired into the dust cloud.

"Missed!" groaned Dick as the man flashed past with a yell. "Oh, sister—do go——"

"No," she said thickly, owing to the swirling alkali cloud enveloping them, "we've shared danger together . . . and we'll face it to the end. Come down, Tony, we've no chance. We'll defy these scoundrels like Braves of the Prairie. Let's give them the defiance war-whoop of the Pawnees. Here they come . . . one . . . two . . . three . . . WHOOH-OOH! WHOOH-AH!"

It was a good effort, but dust choked their tired throats. At sight of Dick's outstretched arm the score of horsemen drew rein on the edge of the dust cloud. As through a fog the children could make out men in 'puncher attire, rifles slung across shoulders; one man wore a head-dress of feathers and held up an object which resembled a bag, and all seemed to be shouting at once and waving arms, hats, lassoes.

"There's nothing to gloat about," said May, "the cowards! A gang of big strong men hounding down three small infants—Sh-h! Listen!"

"Yippee! Yah-hoo!" came in a chorus. "Kio! Kio-oo! cowboy. Give 'em three cheers, lads. Yip—yip—Hooray—y! AND our war-cry. Ya-ya-yah—Kioo—Ya-ya-yah!"

Even then the three children stood still as rag dolls, not daring to hope, not realising the truth, as others arrived and joined in the spree; and as each came up, a cowboy shouted:

"Keep back till the boss comes. Let him be first. Now, lads, once again—three cheers for May, Dick and Tony. Are you ready? Hip—hip——," but the hooray was clipped off sharp, as a large man on a black horse came loping up, dismounted and came running with outstretched arms towards the Crusoes.

"Thank the Good God!" he said. "I can't believe.... Let me see them ... let me feel them first. I'd given them up for dead ... a year ago."

With the cry of "FATHER!" the three little Pawnees fell into his arms.

CHAPTER XIX

THE LONG TRAIL ENDS

THE dust had settled, but not the jollification.

"But, Dad," said Dick, "how did you all change from bandits to . . . cowboys?"

Judge Warner laughed as he stood towering over them: six feet tall and strong as a bison—as many of his hands knew quite well; a stern man, though with a merry blue eye for those who pleased him, and a hard hand for slackers.

"They never chased you at all, son," he said.

"*We* were the riders you saw making for the station."

"We heard shots," said May, looking puzzled. "Why?"

"To attract your attention, my love. We saw you making off like scared bunnies . . . and a fine chase you've given us."

"And we've killed poor old Magpie for nothing," Tony joined in, glancing to where Jim Harris, the foreman, was taking off the mare's saddle and bridle. "What a pity." A playful cowboy had placed the tattered war-bonnet on Tony's head.

"It is a pity," said Mr. Warner, "but better the mare than that grey colt . . . he's got breeding, Dick, you can tell by his hocks and short back. Where did you get him? But perhaps you'd better keep that story for your mother, eh? Now, men, how many prisoners?"

"We're sorry," Jim Harris spoke out, stepping forward a pace, "only two."

"What about the others—Tiger and his gang?"

"Don't you remember, sir, telling us to follow these runaways? When the telegraph operator had described them and said they'd asked how far to Riverside Ranch, and that one was a tall boy, another a little one, and a pretty girl. . . ."

"Ah, yes," said the father, smiling at May's blushing cheeks, "so I did. Well, well—Tiger can wait. Whom did you catch?"

"A Mexican badly wounded, and a gunnie named

Monty Barnett, sir," Harris answered. "Two of the hands have taken them to the ranch."

"Very well," said the judge, "and we'll all return now. Any volunteers to take May?"

There were a score, but Jim settled the matter by lifting her on to his horse. Nineteen, then, made an offer for Tony.

"The Pawnee Brave is my captive," said Mr. Warner with a shake of the head. As for Dick, he was already astride the colt, his own dear Mousie, pal of his adventures, and he had *breeding*, so had said the best judge of horseflesh in Nebraska. Never would he part with Mousie, not for a million dollars.

Riding home!—what heart-stirring words. The alkali flat gave place to green pastures, dotted with cottonwood trees; a stream with cattle cooling their heels; a drove of horses flung up their heads and dashed away, neighing loudly: the sight of their brands—a capital R—provided another thrill; and in the distance the white-fronted ranch buildings and outhouses, surrounded by an orchard and gardens.

The Good News had gone before, and Mrs. Warner was on the verandah watching them ride in: May on the saddle in front of laughing Jim Harris, the happy little Pawnee Brave lively as an eel and half buried in feathers, clutching his bag of treasures in one hand (a cowboy had lifted it from the cactus bush) and waving the other; Dick proud as an Indian warrior on the grey colt. Home—and safety.

Their mother tried to cuddle three at once, but

137

kissed mostly feathers until Dick pulled the Pawnee war-bonnet out of the way.

"It is like being captured by Redskins!" she gasped between kisses. "Are you going to burn me at the stake?"

"We could do with another kind of steak," grinned Dick, feeling hungry.

"Or bacon," twinkled May, and the group of cowboys wondered why the three rescued ones doubled up with laughter.

"Well," said Mr. Warner, as they all sat down to a very late lunch, "you don't appear to have come to much harm in the Pawnee camp; you all look fit and brown as leather. I don't suppose you'll care much for *our* kind of food," indicating with his carving knife the roast beef and vegetables. "Sorry we have no pemmican."

"*We* aren't," smiled Dick, and May agreed.

"Like eating boot soles," said Tony, causing a laugh.

"You mentioned bacon," said Mrs. Warner soberly, looking puzzled. "We have plenty in the larder—if——"

By the time the three hungry ones had explained the joke, the first course was finished and while waiting for the ginger pudding and sauce, Dick said, "By the way, sister, you didn't tell us how you managed to get made into bacon—you'd got to where you climbed up into the last freight car——"

"There's not much to add," May continued her

story. "The sound of a shot awoke me and as I'd no desire to meet the bandits, I popped into that empty crate and wriggled under the straw with the sack on top. Through a chink I saw a man climb into the freight car and watched his mouth water as he read the word BACON stencilled on the side. Then along came a cart and two men lowered the crate into it, none too gently either, and one of them said, as he hammered in a few nails with his boot heel, 'This is a weighty piece of bacon'—the impudence!

"So, like Brer Rabbit, I lay low, and then through a crack I saw a tall, handsome boy standing at the door of a cattle truck with a little boy peeping through his legs."

"How strange," said Dick, straight faced but bubbling inwardly. "I wonder who they were?"

"Horrid tramps," May went on, having fine fun. "I heard them say so, and the big handsome boy— something after your style, Dicky—but much braver, because when a fierce bandit came along, the tall, handsome boy said, 'Is there a dining-car on this train? I rather fancy a slice of bacon——"

"I . . . didn't," blushed Dick. "I mean—he wouldn't dare say that to a robber."

"Well," she rattled on, "I couldn't hear very clearly owing to the straw pricking my ears; however, the boys were told to climb on to the cart and sat dangling their legs on my crate. I tickled the little boy's legs with a straw——"

"Ah! Don't you remember, Tony," Dick took up

the tale. "I said there was something alive in the crate and suggested a bear-cub, but you said . . . monkey."

"That's right," Tony nodded, trying to hide a broad grin with his hand.

"Um!" May chuckled. "Perhaps it was a monkey —it has a long *tale* anyway. . . ."

When the mirth had died down she concluded quickly, "You know the rest. When we arrived at the cave and I saw Mr. Throat Slitter sharpening his knife, I just hunched up my back and out came the nails."

"And out came sister just in time," said Dick. "You deserve an honour feather."

"And so does Tony," said May. "He saved the miners' camp."

The recounting of Tony's brave deed lasted through the sweet course and he was patted on the back by Mr. Warner; then Dick asked: "How did you know Tiger Murrell's gang had held up the train, Dad?"

"The telegraph operator had just time to flash the warning to Riverside Halt before being held up and his instruments broken, which reminds me—I've to interview that young bandit fellow. You may leave the table, children. Ah, here comes the foreman."

"The Mexican can't be moved, sir," said Harris, "but Barnett's all right . . . just had a meal. Shall I bring him in?"

"Yes," the Judge replied. "What's the matter with your hand?"

Jim eyed the bandage on his left fingers. "Nothing serious, sir, a brute of a dog came nosing around and wouldn't be shooed away. He'd already mauled two of ours and when I went to grab his collar—a fancy Indian one—he snapped at me."

Tony pricked up his ears. "What kind of a dog, Mr. Harris?"

"A sort of a wolfy Indian cur——" He paused as Tony gave a wild "Hurrah!" and rushed to the door, with Dick and May at his heels.

It was indeed Wolfie, tired, sore footed and hungry, and he yapped with joy when three pairs of arms encircled his fancy collar. It had taken a lot of trail sniffing to locate the ranch, but he had done it and was soon worrying a beef bone with canine contentment.

141

CHAPTER XX

THE ROUND-UP OF TIGER'S GANG

WHILE this happy reunion was taking place, Judge Warner was interviewing the captured bandit.

"How old are you, Barnett?" asked the Judge gravely.

"Twenty, sir, next month."

"Um! The tenth of October is my little boy's birthday, but I don't think *you'll* be at liberty to enjoy yours. Even if you escape the rope, you'll be jailed. We are determined to put down this robbing of trains . . . and murder."

The bandit shrugged his shoulders. "I'm not one of the gang, sir. I've done nothing worse than help to brand stolen stock."

"You were caught with Murrell's gang and must take the consequences. You were studying for a veterinary surgeon, I hear?"

"Yes, sir, but failed . . . so went cowpunching until a horse broke my thigh. I was out on the ranges and Murrell's men helped me . . . so I allowed them to use my shack. This is a new part of the world to me. I didn't know until just now that you were Judge Warner. Maybe this I.O.U. would interest you?" He placed the note on the desk.

Mr. Warner looked astonished. He was in a fix:

indebted to a bandit for helping his children, perhaps saving their lives, even if indirectly.

"I'll settle the debt, Barnett. All the borrowed goods will be returned to you."

"Would it be possible to give me another chance, sir? I'll promise to keep away from Murrell."

"I doubt it, but will speak to the sheriff about you. There's one item in your favour: you attended to the wounded telegraph operator."

Three weeks later at Riverside Ranch, preparation was being made for Tony's eighth birthday party. He had issued numerous invitations to children to come to the Pawnee Pow-wow and Dance, fancy dress (meaning Indian) preferred.

Then at daybreak on the morning of Tony's birthday a message came from the sheriff asking Mr. Warner to send his cowboys to Pine Gulch, because information had been received that Murrell's gang intended holding up the train carrying gold to pay the railroad builders.

"Now, cheer up, my brave Pawnee," said Mr. Warner, noting Tony's glum expression, "we'll all be back before party time and if we capture Tiger you shall have him for a birthday present," he joked.

During the afternoon the Rancher's posse came galloping back.

"Captured the whole gang," said the Judge. "The sheriff has them all jailed—Murrell included."

"Was Barnett there?" asked Dick.

"No. One of the bandits told me that Monty has

gone into another State—to be veterinary surgeon on a ranch."

At twilight that same day a stranger rode up to the barn where the party was being held, and asked to see Tony Warner.

"Barnett sends Many Happy Returns and this bundle," said the stranger, when Tony appeared.

It was such a huge parcel that Dick had to help his brother to open it. Out rolled a beautiful bear-skin with head attached.

"Ooo-oo!" cried Tony. "It's the one we left at Monty's cabin. Please thank Mr. Barnett for curing the skin."